SIMON FAYTER
AND THE TITAN'S GROAN

Austin J. Bailey

Austin Bailey
www.austinjbailey.com
Email address: austin@austinjbailey.com

Editing and interior book design by:
Crystal Watanabe
www.pikkoshouse.com

Printed in the United States of America

To Crystal, who knows *everything.*[1]

---

1 Including the fact that if your character loses his pants in outer space, he can't magically have them back again five chapters later. Also, the difference between a pun and an idiom, the sound a vintage rotary telephone makes when it hits someone in the head, how to spell pneumonoultramicroscopicsilicovolcanokoniosis, what the D2 and C3 knobs actually do, and what I wrote last year. As it turns out, that kind of stuff is more important than you'd think.

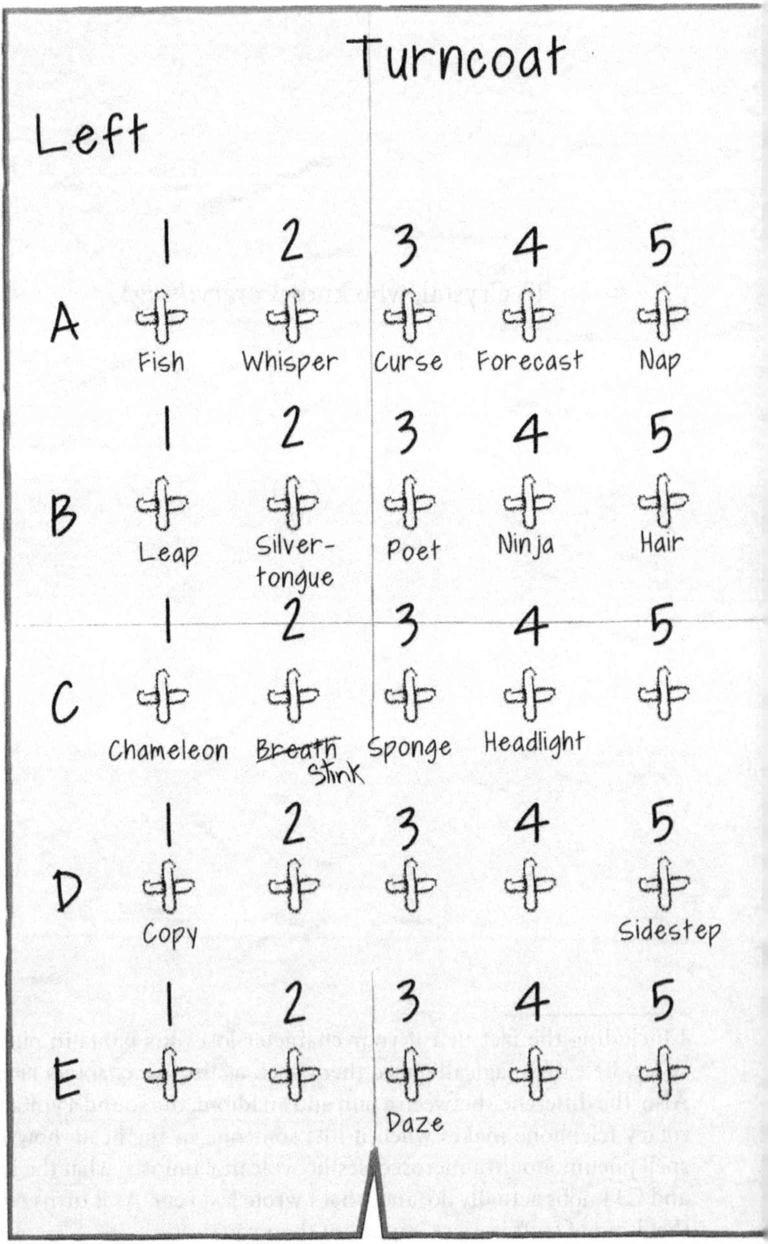

Turncoat

Left

	1	2	3	4	5
A	Fish	Whisper	Curse	Forecast	Nap
B	Leap	Silver-tongue	Poet	Ninja	Hair
C	Chameleon	~~Breath~~ Stink	Sponge	Headlight	
D	Copy				Sidestep
E			Daze		

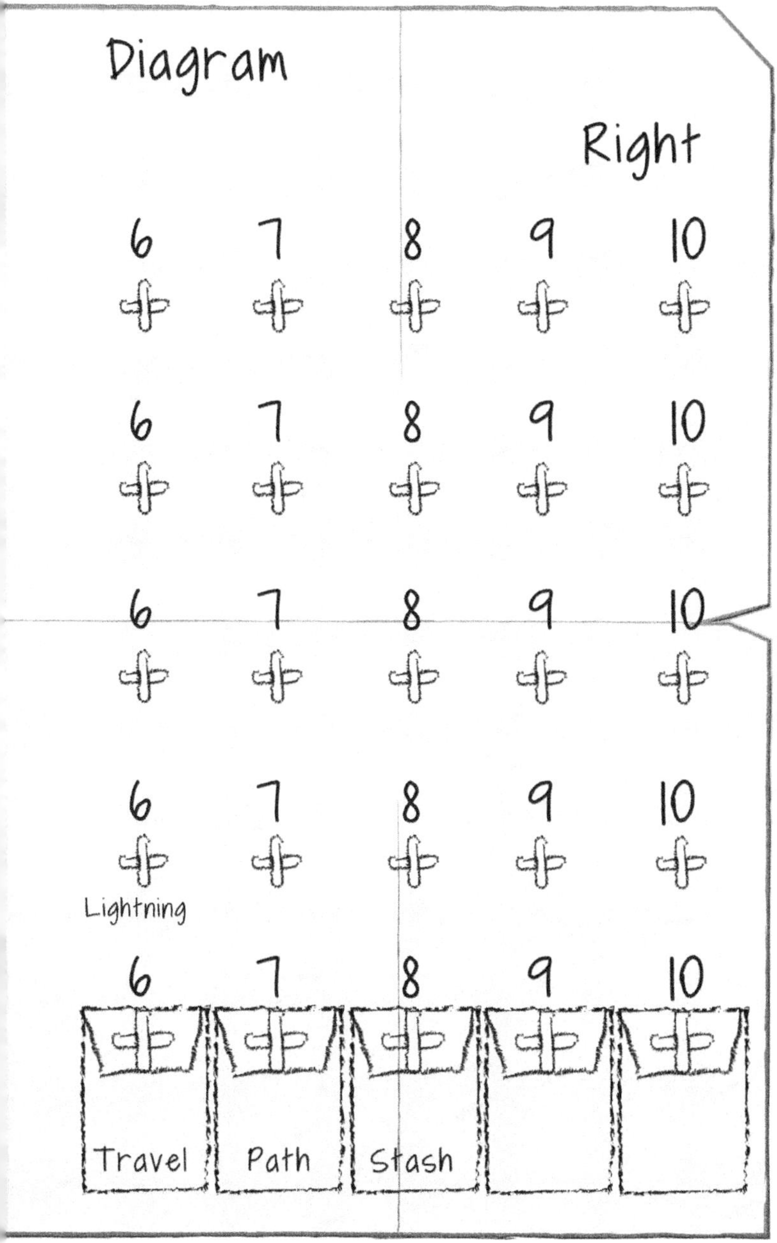

Diagram

Right

6 7 8 9 10

6 7 8 9 10

6 7 8 9 10

6 7 8 9 10

Lightning

6 7 8 9 10

Travel Path Stash

TABLE OF CONTENTS

PROLOGUE

Hindsight is 20/20. [2]

—Al Kindzapeople

Ioden Bright wrapped the tattered remains of his pink bathrobe around himself and stepped cautiously onto the field of death.

That was what he had come to call it these last three days. The field of death.

Three days! Was that all it had been? It had started when he was brushing his teeth—minding his own business, by the way. The next moment, he was standing beside that… that *awful* child. The one everybody was fawning over as if he were the number-one chief stud hunk genius hero king of the universe. Simon blah blah blah *Fayter.*

"Simon Fayter," he grumbled under his breath. "Simon

2 This common idiom simply means that it's easier to evaluate choices after they've already happened. The saying originated sometime after the Snellen chart—a big wall chart with random letters presented in descending size order to test visual acuity—was developed in 1862 by Herman Snellen. This is not to be confused with the *Smellin'* Chart—a big wall chart with random scratch-and-sniff boxes presented in descending smelliness order to test olfactory acuity, which was developed in 1863 by Herman Smellin. No relation.

Faker. Simon *Farter.* Simon *Flunker!*"

With each name, he took another step, staring around himself in a sort of wild terror, eyes wide in anticipation. Any minute now, they would strike. They would drive him back up that blasted cliff to wait out the day, starving and sun baked, just as they had yesterday, and the day before, and the day before that.

A twig snapped under his bare foot, and he spun around, sure they were sneaking up behind him. But no. He was still safe.

Safe.

He looked longingly toward the sea. If he could just make it off this bleeding field, over the hill, and onto the beach, he might stand a chance against them. He was a formidable wizard, but magical strength slackened just as physical strength did when a man was denied adequate food and rest. It could be that this last try would mean his death. Perhaps it was foolish to attempt it. Hard to know now. No doubt the wisdom of his choice would be clear later. Hindsight and all that.

Just then, it came: a soft, padding sound from the left and right. The field upon which he stood was perhaps two hundred yards wide and skirted on either side by a line of trees. The cliff upon which he had been forced to shelter after his numerous retreats was behind him. Ahead lay the hill, the beach, the sea.

The padding sound grew louder, and he burst into a run. If he didn't make it, he wouldn't have time or strength to retreat. He reached the foot of the hill and leaped up as dozens, no, *hundreds* of giant man-eating Yap rabbits burst from the tree line. They thundered after him, filling the field. They were almost upon him when he reached the top of the hill and careened down the other side, laughing wildly. He felt desperate, manic, ready to be free or die.

Then there was sand beneath his feet. Sweet, wonderful sand. And he was still alive! If he had been stronger, better fed, better rested, perhaps a *bit* more powerful, he could have done this from his place on top of the cliff. He could have thrown stones or even lifted himself into the air and flown, but now, *now* he was here. Touching the sand. And for a Bright, one who knew the subtle and complicated art of telekinesis, touching the subject to be moved made the process so much easier. Easy enough for even a half-starved, half-naked, sleep-deprived history teacher to weaponize ten thousand tons of sand.

Ioden turned on the spot, raised his hands in triumph, and began to laugh. Sand rose around him in a swirling cloud as he turned to face his pursuers. The first twenty man-sized killer bunnies to reach the beach were vaporized by a wall of sand moving at the speed of sound.

The next wave was buried, beaten back, thrown into the air, or driven away by sand animals born from the imagination of a desperate wizard. He had never done anything, *anything*, as impressive as this before. He must be controlling thousands, millions, billions of sand particles at the same time. He had heard of great wizards working magic like this, but he'd never attempted anything of the sort. He'd never known he could.

Unfortunately, the rabbits that were not killed instantly by his sand monsters simply grew larger and larger, stronger and faster. There were, in fact, more of the beasts than he had entirely accounted for. Soon they began to crowd him, forcing him and his sand creatures back toward the ocean.

But no matter. He shifted his focus to the sand beneath his feet, and it burst out of the ground, lifting him high into the air on a hundred-foot tower.

"Bwahahaha!" he laughed manically down at the frothing mass of rabbits. "Get me now!"

There were hundreds of them down there. Thousands leaping about in a wild frenzy. Even in the morning sunlight, it was unnerving. Ioden leaned through a sandy embrasure[3] and willed his giant tower slowly out into the sea. Soon there was a hundred yards of water separating his tower from the beach, and the rabbits were left to pace back and forth, staring out at him.

"Now what?" he wondered aloud. The sun was shining, the sea crashed upon itself here and there in peaceful waves, and there was a pleasant breeze. He was free. But free to do what? He would survive now, but for what? Yap rabbits only lived in one place (everyone knew that), which meant that he was on the island of Yap, in the Sea of Timidity, not far from the Star of Dark Haven. If there were places less visited, more cursed, or harder to escape

3 The top of a castle wall or turret generally has an up-down, up-down pattern to its shape (to make it more defensible), like intermittent gaps between teeth. The teeth, or high parts in this case, are called merlons, and the gaps are called embrasures.

from, he didn't know of any. Even if he had a spacesail ship and a crew to man it, he might not ever make it home. But he didn't have those things. All he had was a pile of sand.

A sea bird flew by, and he shot it out of the air with a sand bullet. Then he hovered the dead bird over to himself and set it roasting on a sand spit, set on four sand sticks over a magic fire. At least now he wouldn't starve.

He let the tower melt into the sea as he pondered his situation. Soon it was only a few feet high, and he found himself staring into the water around him. So much water. Endless, like the expanse of space that no doubt separated him from...everything.

He blinked, watching a school of strange fish as they circled his tower. At first he thought they were tiny sharks because of the triangular fins sticking out of the water, but then one poked its head out, and he was surprised to see that the fin came straight out of the top of the fish's head like a hat. Below the fin, they each had a single yellow cyclops eye staring out at him with interest. They swam sideways, always keeping their faces toward him, the little fins circling, circling.

His tower bumped something then—he must have still been moving it through the water without realizing it—and a long shadow fell across him. He turned to see a large rock outcropping. It jutted out of the ocean, fifty yards high, and looked, strangely enough, very much like the little head-fins on those fish. No, it was at least seventy yards high. No, eighty. Was it growing before his eyes?

He stood up in amazement as he realized that it *was*

growing before his eyes. Rising up, up out of the ocean. The eye came next—twenty feet across, breaking the surface of the water and staring down at him. The mouth came after that, open, gaping, filled with ten thousand pointed teeth.

Ioden gulped, staring up at it. Perhaps this had been a bad idea after all. As usual, hindsight was 20/20. He got to his feet and gestured at the little school of fish, which was now rapidly retreating from his tower. "What a, err... lovely family you have," he said pleasantly.

The fish monster said nothing, only opened its mouth wider and tilted slowly over him.

"SIMMMMMMOON FAYYYYYTERRRRR!" Ioden screamed as the great fish crashed down.

And then it swallowed him, his tower, his half-roasted sea bird, and a great deal of ocean water besides.

One thorn of experience is worth a whole wilderness of warning.

—James Russell Lowell[4]

Technically speaking, our story begins on a *lucky* day, although it was certainly the most unlucky lucky day I've ever had.

By the way, don't tell me you read the prologue again. That's *three* times now, isn't it? Well, if you are wondering what Ioden has to do with this story, the answer is nothing. I do feel bad (okay, not really) that he keeps getting tugged around to strange places at inopportune times, so now and then—once a book, maybe—we will be checking in on him to see how he's faring. At any rate, I believe I told you at the end of Book 2 that Book 3 picks up right where we left off, and so it does:

I turned E6 (*Travel*), and at once the horrible scene[5]

4 One of the first popular American poets. He inspired Mark Twain to write characters who spoke with funny accents.

5 You remember: Bast, Hawk, the Tike, Drake, Tessa, and myself, locked in the soultrap, thousands of bloodhounds trying to break through and eat us, the soultrap opening to let them in, and me faced with the horrible decision of which of my friends to abandon to their

vanished before my eyes. My friends were gone. Drake, who at the last second had grabbed Tessa's arm and reached for me across the distance between us as if to pull me toward him, was gone. Abandoning him hurt most of all, because he knew where I was going, and he had wanted to come.

Of course, if I had taken the time to think through my situation more carefully, I would have realized that I could have brought almost everyone with me and still accomplished my goal of running away from my tough decision. But if I had taken the time to think through my situation more carefully, I would have wasted a few seconds—not more than five, given the genius nature of my mind—in which time the soultrap would have collapsed, and we would have all been slaughtered by bloodhounds. Not very nice. So yes, I acted without thinking[6] and abandoned all of my friends.

Kind of.

---

death. What's that, you say? You don't know what I am talking about? Then *you,* sir or madam, have failed to read Books 1 and 2—a crime I find completely inexcusable. Didn't you see the little 3 on the side of this book? I suggest you go begin at the beginning, because I don't have time to bring you up to speed. I know. That is very rude of me. If my rudeness offends you, my advice is to feed this book to your pet chinchilla, and then go find some *other* wizarding autobiography about a genius kid with a magic jacket and awesome friends—thick with magical mayhem, unpredictable plot twists, humor, sarcasm, and superfluous (but charming) footnotes. Oh, wait. There *aren't* any other books like that…

6 A phenomenon common among my kind. My kind being *teenagers,* of course. Not *super awesome unbroken wizards who can whistle in three languages.* Obviously, in that sense, I am without peer.

I mean, I *was* planning to go back for them…

Anyway, I turned E6, and everything vanished.

It felt like getting hit by a train. The world was gone and something huge and invisible smashed into my body, flattening me. I went from boy to pancake to boy again in the blink of an eye. When it was over, and I had been successfully transported across the galaxy and into the distant past, I opened my eyes to see the ancient city of Tarinea stretched out before me, blazing white under the light of two suns.

I was standing on the edge of a bluff—the same one upon which I had previously appeared—and looking down on what I now knew to be one of the most famous cities in wizarding history.

Tarinea lay in a fertile valley. At the center of the city was a huge white pyramid. The structure was easily ten city blocks wide at the base and just as high, its white sides gleaming like a polished gem. The city itself was divided into four quadrants, stretching out as if from the four points of the central pyramid.

The top-left one was occupied by simple stone houses, the bottom-left one with graves, the top-right section with fields and farmland, and the bottom-right with a tangled clump of industrial buildings. The city was so large that I couldn't see to the far side, but I could tell that around the perimeter, like a magnificent frame, stood a white wall hundreds of feet high.

I looked around me, taking in the beauty of the city beyond, the pleasant warmth of the rocks beneath my boots, and the peaceful quiet of the mountain. I was quite alone, and suddenly quite safe, which made me think of my friends back on Cathagorous, trapped beneath Rone's tomb. A monolithic sense of guilt hit me. How could I have abandoned them like that?

At that moment, all such thoughts were silenced as my mind became overwhelmed by an incredibly itchy nose. I sneezed and doubled over, scratching my nose. Inside, outside, upside down—it itched *everywhere*. And yet I couldn't seem to scratch the source of the itch. It was horrible.

I know what you're thinking. You're thinking about my code. The sacred magical promises that I had made to the Zohar:

I will be my best self
I will honor my word
I will help those I can
I will never give up

You're thinking that by abandoning my friends and trying to hide from the tough decision I had to make, I was giving up and not being my best self. Yes, yes. Congratulations. You're very smart.

Eventually the itching subsided for a while, and I looked around. I heard...music. Whistling, to be more precise. It was coming from somewhere ahead of me. No, *beneath* me.

I peered over the side of the bluff and looked down

toward where I knew the entrance of a small cave was hidden below—the cave in which, on my previous visit, I had seen a boy crying. I lowered myself over the edge and began to descend the cliff face, just as I had done before. This time, I stopped short. There were several signs bolted to the rock face, positioned so that someone climbing down it couldn't help but see them. I don't know how I had managed to miss them last time. They read: "The penalty for disturbing the cave of Balgrotha is death by torture. You have been warned."

Hmm...

That sounded sort of serious. Then again, I had seen that kid in there before, and now someone—no doubt the same boy—was whistling, just hanging out in there, so it probably wasn't as big a deal as these signs made out. I would just go down and take a look. It wasn't like I was going to *disturb* anything.

I came to the lower ledge and edged along it once again until I reached the point over the cave. Then I lay down on my stomach and carefully hung over the side, peering into the cave below. Before I could see anything, I felt Kylanthus slip out of its scabbard. Luckily I managed to grab the hilt just before it tumbled a hundred feet to who knows where. Breathing hard, I rolled back to safety, clutching the sword tightly.

Great! I had barely even arrived, and I was accidentally dropping my magical sword off the first cliff I saw. Just to be safe, I turned E8 (*Stash*), and Kylanthus disappeared into the magical compartment inside my coat. Better safe than sorry.

I hung over the edge once more and had a look.

Sure enough, the boy was there. He was just sitting now, legs crossed, looking very relaxed. He whistled to pass the time, apparently waiting for something. Or someone.

As I watched, two figures, cloaked in red, emerged from the shadows behind him. They stepped from the black bowels of the cave, moving in complete silence, their faces covered in ornately carved golden masks shaped like the faces of wild predators—a howling wolf and a snarling jaguar. They crept toward him, tall and menacing, holding long black spears.

"Watch out!" I shouted. Or rather, I meant to, for just then a hand grabbed a fistful of my hair and yanked me to my feet.

"What are you doing here?" a voice growled from behind me.

"Uh, I don't know?" I said honestly.

Another hand grabbed my belt, and I was thrown in a high arc, up and over the cliff face I had climbed down. I landed hard on the rock above and looked around for my enemy. Below, I heard laughter, then a scream.

Slowly, a figure in a heavy red cloak appeared, rising through the air above the edge of the cliff. It had a golden mask like the others—a warthog with wide tusks and bared teeth. The figure hovered in midair, then stepped onto the rocky bluff, towering over me.

I reached inside the turncoat, but his spear lashed out, smacking my arm just above the elbow. I felt a flash of pain, and my arm went limp, flopping to my side.

"The penalty for disturbing the cave of Balgrotha," the red-cloaked thing growled from behind the golden mask, "is death by torture."

"Oh, bother…" I mumbled. I wasn't off to a very good start.

The spear zipped through the air toward my head, spinning madly. I wondered briefly whether the butt or the point would hit me first. Then, everything went dark.

To know that we know what we know, and to know that we do not know what we do not know, that is true knowledge.

—Copernicus[7]

When I woke up, I was tortured. It wasn't what you think, though.

I mean, I *was* in a damp underground chamber with a dirt floor, a tiny bit of moonlight filtering through a long, narrow pipe in the roof, and there *was* a mysterious substance smeared on the walls that I suspected to be blood. Also, there *was* a large one-eyed bald guy with a stained leather apron and a case full of torture devices. Other than all *that*, though, it wasn't what you think.

For example, the first thing he said to me after I regained consciousness was, "Hoh ULLg?"

"What?" I said, touching the side of my head. There was a big welt there from getting clocked by the butt of the spear.

"Hohhh Ullg?" he repeated carefully.

---

7 A fifteenth-century astronomer who argued (correctly) that the sun, rather than the earth, was the center of our solar system. He was really, *really* good at math.

"How old?" I guessed.

My torturer clapped with enthusiasm. "Yahhhh!"

"Of course I would get the torturer who can't speak," I said rudely.

"Clshorrrry," he said. Then he opened his mouth and pointed to where his tongue had probably been once, long ago, before it had been removed.

"Gah," I said, wincing. "Well…I'm thirteen."

"Oooo," he said, sitting back onto a wobbly three-legged stool and opening his case. "Gooood. Wey doongh[8] hurgh schid[9]ren."

"Oh…good," I said, eyeing him as he rummaged through his instruments. "If you don't mind my asking, what are you looking for in there, if not something to hurt me with?"

"Feagher."

"Come again?"

He withdrew a strange-looking glove and put it on his left hand. It was completely covered in short black bristly feathers. With the other hand, he held a long, very slender brown feather.

"*Feathers*," I said. "And what, pray tell, are you going to do with those?"

"No wohrry. No huuht. Ony ghoghure."

"Only torture?" I clarified.

He nodded.

---

8 It's really hard to make a "T" sound without a tongue. "L" too, for that matter.

9 It's really hard to make a "D" sound without a tongue too, but somehow he managed that. Go figure…

"Oh, good. However, I should tell you that I'm happy to just spill the beans on whatever it is you want to know—not that I know anything, of course." I attempted to reach into the turncoat, but my hands were bound tightly behind me. I groped for my power mentally, hoping desperately to summon the Midnight Blue or something, but there was nothing there. Sad, really, that you could incapacitate the so-called "most powerful" wizard ever, simply by tying his hands behind his back. I'd have to work on that.

He shrugged. "Schalk waygher. Now, ghoghure."

"Talk later..." I mumbled as he advanced, holding the feather before him like a surgeon with his scalpel. Now torture. Lovely.

In case you weren't aware, there are any number of ways to torture a person without actually harming them physically. For example, sleep deprivation. Just shine a light in someone's face, jostle them about a bit, and make sure they don't sleep. After four or five days, they'll tell you anything. Of course, that causes delusions, paranoia, psychosis, hallucinations, and eventually death, so I guess you can't say it's harmless.

However, in the ancient city of Tarinea, the King's Guard (my pleasant, red-cloaked captors) actually did have a firm policy of not hurting children (at least not directly), so I got the tickle treatment. The most ticklish spot on the human body is, of course, the inside of the nose.[10]

---

10 As many unsuspecting wielders of the fabled "nose-hair trimmer" learn the hard way.

Let me tell you, having someone put a feather up there[11] is as uncomfortable as anything I have ever experienced. I laughed, then cried, then screamed, then passed out. Twelve times. Eventually, I was given the chance to talk to someone—a different man, one with two eyes, two ears, and a tongue—and I told him everything I knew. I told him about my childhood. I told him my earliest memories, my deepest fears, all the secrets I knew, about the bloodstones, the Circle of Eight, Rellik, Rone, the turncoat, the breaking of magical powers, and my destiny to save the world. I even told them that I was Luke Skywalker, that I knew where the stolen Death Star plans were hidden, and that these *were* the droids they were looking for. What can I say?[12]

Naturally, since Tarinea existed before wizard powers ever broke in the first place, and before the bloodstones were ever given to Rok (and they'd never even seen *Star Wars*), the King's Guard thought that I was either crazy or lying.

So, they ghoghured me again.

It was a lovely couple of days.

Interestingly, the Zohar didn't torture me through wild nose itching at all while I was *actually* being tortured

11 Of course, you should *never* put anything up your nose, or in your ears or eyes. It could actually be very dangerous. The ancient Egyptians regularly sucked people's brains out through their noses after they died. Think about it: If your brain can come *out* of your nose, you should really be careful about what you put *in* your nose. Think about *that* next time you pick…

12 I'm not proud of it, but I can be a bit of a coward at times. We know this.

by wild nose itching. Small mercies. The irony was not lost on me, however, and I spent many excruciating hours pondering how I had given up, taken the easy way out, and not been my best self. Strange, then, how the path I was on (spoiler alert) would lead me to fulfilling my destiny. Sometimes the path to our destiny is achieved despite our actions, or perhaps even *because* we have not been our best selves. Herein lies one of the great mysteries of life. Hence the quote at the beginning of this chapter.

When it was all over, and they determined that I was delusional, they threw me into a different underground cell. This one had people in it already. There was an old guy staring up an air pipe in the center of the room and a middle-aged woman with no teeth who was stacking rocks in the corner and singing softly to herself.

"One atop the other, up and up we go. No one lives forever, sorrow we will sow." There was also a third person. One I recognized.

"You!" I shouted at the pointy-featured boy from the cave. My hands were still tied behind my back, but I got to my feet awkwardly. "You got me into this mess! Where are we?"

He had been leaning against the wall of the cell, looking rather nonchalant, but now he scowled. "You got snatched too, eh? Well, that's not my problem. Maybe you should have thought of that before you went and *spied* on people." His intelligent eyes were hard, unyielding.

So he *did* remember me watching him as he cried. I thought about bringing it up, asking him what he had been so sad about, but he looked like he might rip my face off if I did that. "Sorry," I said. "I didn't mean to, honest. I was just sort of...drawn to that cave place. What is it? Is that why we got caught? Because of the signs?"

He cracked a smile then, as if at a joke, but when I didn't smile back, he looked confused. "Good Garamond,[13] kid! You really don't know why you're here, do you?"

I was about to tell him that I didn't appreciate being called a kid by someone clearly younger than myself, but just then the cell door banged open, and in walked one of the tall red-cloaked King's Guards, this one with a lion mask, complete with a shining mane.

"You are all here," he began in a guttural voice, "because of the heinous[14] crimes that you have committed." He looked at the old man. "Stealing food from the

---

13 One of the hardest parts of writing kids' books is, of course, never swearing. The sad truth is, kids don't actually have the best language all the time—especially ancient, troubled wizard kids. In fact, kids sometimes do swear or say other bad things. But you can't write that. And so, history is altered (as it should be), *softened*, so as not to offend tender ears. Still, it makes writing tricky, because we, the writers, must invent strange and random (preferably funny) substitutions for swear words. In this book, I have decided (since this *is* a *book* full of *writing* and such) that the swear words will all be names of fonts. Garamond is, of course, one of the greats, and the very font in which the original paperback version of this book was set. If you are a child, or just a conscientious adult, and desire to clean up your language, you are welcome to use my swearfonts in your day-to-day life, although there is an argument to be made about expletives of any form (swear word or not) being the desperate recourse of the weak minded and not a respectable form of expression at all... It's a silly argument, though. *Garamonding* silly.

14 Utterly odious, repulsive, unpleasantly wicked.

archbishop." He looked at the fidgety woman. "Feeding a child that is not your own." He looked at me, and his voice rose in anger. "Disturbing the cave of Balgrotha!"

The man and woman both gasped, looking at me in horror. Evidently they hadn't realized what a hardened, black-hearted criminal they had been alone with for the last two minutes.

"Wait a minute," I said, glancing at the boy. "What about him? It's *his* fault I'm here in the first place!"

The King's Guard shoved me backward with remarkable strength, and I thudded against the cell wall. "FOR YOUR CRIMES," he went on, "you shall be tortured forever."

I sighed.

"Or..." He looked around at us with deliberate slowness. "You can choose life beyond pain. However short that may be..."

"I'm intrigued," I said, stepping forward. "I choose life beyond pain. Get me out of here."

"Though it pains me to agree with a foolish child," my new annoying friend said, "I, too, choose life beyond pain."

The old man stepped forward as well, but the woman kept stacking rocks in the corner. The King's Guard, perhaps wondering whether she had heard him, knocked over her stack of rocks with his spear. She screamed and gathered the rocks back into a pile at her feet. "I've seen your foul arenas!" she spat. "Your monsters and your mayhem! I prefer to die here, with dignity, however long it may take."

"Fine," the guard said. He stood the three of us in a line and tied our feet together with lengths of rope so that none of us could escape without dragging the others. Then he slowly led us out.

I happened to be in the back of the line, so I glanced at the woman before the door closed. She was looking at me with an unexpected expression on her face. Was that pity? She was the one who had chosen death by torture, wasn't she? But she looked away before I could be sure and resumed slowly stacking her rocks.

"One atop the other, up and up we go. No one lives forever, sorrow we will sow."

The door screeched to a close behind me, and we walked slowly into darkness, dragging our feet on the rocky ground. I wondered then, just what I had gotten myself into, and if perhaps I had made a mistake.

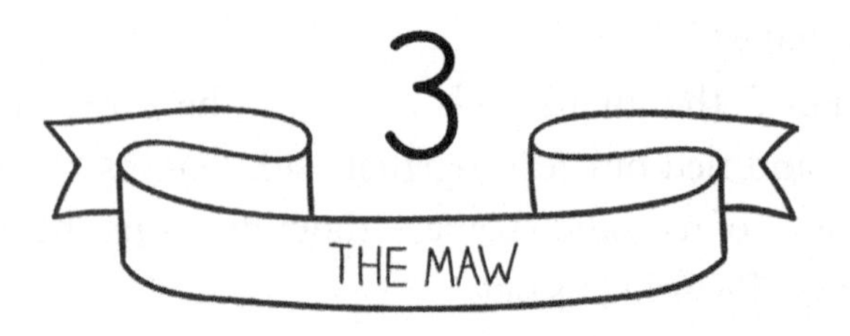

Out of suffering have emerged the strongest souls; the most massive characters are seared with scars.

—Kahlil Gibran[15]

There was no preparation, no preamble. No little meeting in a room full of weapons where we got to pick our poison or figure out what was going on. The guard simply took us to a door in the side of a curving wall, unlocked it, and shoved us in.

I stumbled into a dark arena.

Actually, "arena" is a bit of a stretch. At first glance, I thought I was in some sort of pit. The ground was covered in soft dirt, like a tilled garden, and the wide, curving walls were of black stone and went straight up at least two hundred feet. Soft light filtered down from above so that it

---

15 Born in Lebanon in the late 1800s, Khalil Gibran is the third-bestselling poet of all time. He is best known for his book *The Prophet*, which says (among other things) "When love beckons to you, follow him,/though his ways are hard and steep./And when his wings enfold you, yield to him,/though the sword hidden among his pinions may wound you./And when he speaks to you believe in him./Though his voice may shatter your dreams as the north wind lays waste the garden./For even as love crowns you so shall he crucify you. Even as he is for your growth, so is he for your pruning.

was just light enough to see the ground in front of me. The pit felt large—at least two football fields wide—and was apparently empty. It was deadly quiet. For a moment, all I heard was the sound of my own breathing. Then a sound came from somewhere far above us. It reminded me of the tide coming in, but it took me a minute to realize that it was people. People cheering.

"Run!" the boy shouted at me, then sprinted away, following the wall to my left.

The old man had dropped to his knees and was praying in a hoarse whisper: "Forgive me for a life misled. Make me ready to be dead."

"Oh boy," I muttered. "This can't be good."

With some difficulty (and looking much like a confused yoga practitioner), I reached into the turncoat with my bound hands and turned E8 (*Stash*). Kylanthus materialized in midair before me, and I let it drop to the ground. Then I kneeled and cut myself free. I rose, sword in hand, just as the ground began to shake.

From the shadows on the far side of the pit, a great beast emerged. It was twenty feet high at the shoulders and vaguely resembled a supersized rhinoceros, except that it had two heads and two horns (one on each end), and its giant mouth was on its underside, facing the ground, like a great, inverted Venus flytrap. Also, it was magenta, and while I'd never thought of magenta as being a scary color, it suddenly seemed quite menacing. Something prickled in my mind at seeing the beast—something *other* than panic, that is. Although I had obviously never seen a giant, two-headed, belly-mouth, magenta rhino before, it was strangely familiar to me.

The beast reared back on its hind legs and roared, spreading the huge mouth wide to reveal teeth like giant rakes.

I backed up until I hit the wall, then looked around. I don't know what I was hoping to find. A way out, I suppose, or perhaps a rocket-propelled grenade launcher. But of course, there was just dirt, like before.

The old man was running now, so I decided I might as well join him. He was moving at a good clip, but I knew I could catch him. That way, at least neither of us would have to be alone when we got eaten. The beast spotted us, of course, and the ground shook as it raced toward us, bellowing another roar.

A dust devil spun along beside me as I neared the man—no doubt kicked up by the beast's sudden rampage—and I wiped dirt out of my eyes, blinking. I almost tripped over the old man then; he had tripped and fallen. I reached down to lift him up, but the dust devil had stopped right behind me, and just then a pair of thin arms popped out of it and wrapped themselves around my waist. With a jerk, they pulled me into the swirling dirt.

It was strangely quiet inside the column of dust, so the boy's voice seemed abnormally loud beside me. "Keep moving! We are inside an illusion."

I kept pace beside him as he jogged away from where the beast had stopped. The dust swirled around us all the while.

"What about the old man?" I said. "Let's go back for him."

"Too late," the boy said.

"What?" I glanced over my shoulder and saw the beast standing where I had been a few seconds earlier. Sure enough, the man was gone. The beast's long belly-lips shivered then, and it let out a ground-shaking belch.

"Ah, geez," I said, cringing.

"Nothing like starting the day with a bit of violence," the boy said brightly. "Better him than us, I say."

We reached the wall and put our backs to it. I looked at my companion then. He was a bit shorter than me, with a clever look about him, and I was surprised to see that he didn't look all that afraid. It was more like he was *excited.*

He caught me studying him and offered his hand. "Tavronan," he said. "Friends call me Tav."

"Simon," I said. "Friends call me Simon."

"Yeah, well"—he gestured at my sword—"are you any good with that thing, Simon?"

"Not really," I admitted. "At least, not good enough for this. What *is* that thing? What's going on?"

"That *thing*," he said, "is called a humdrungelob. And what's going on is a slave execution." He gestured back and forth between us. "We're the slaves."

At the word "humdrungelob," my subconscious did a little backflip that I didn't quite understand. I knew something about humdrungelwhatsits, didn't I?

"We're slaves?" I asked to keep the conversation going.

He scratched his head. "Only if we kill the monster.

Otherwise, we're lunch."

"But why?"

He gave me a dubious[16] look. "Don't tell me you've never been to the Maw before. You know, slave executions? Titan clashes? It's Tarinea's favorite pastime!"

"I'm not from around here."

"Ah," he said. "Me neither. Just visiting. Speaking of visitors…" He pointed, and we sprinted away as the humdrungelob rampaged toward us.

"Can it see us?" I shouted over the sound of its footfalls.

"No," Tav called back. "Might be able to smell us, though. We can't hide forever."

"What's your plan?" I asked as we took shelter behind a small bump in the outer wall. The humdrungelob had slowed its pace and was heaving its horned head this way and that, working its way slowly toward us.

The boy grinned at me and blew a lock of blond hair out of his eyes. "What makes you think I have a plan?"

"Well, you're here on purpose, aren't you? I assume you trespassed at that cave hoping to be caught, and

---

16 *Suspicious.* By the way, if you feel like these definitions are patronizing because you already know what the difficult words mean, please remember that these books are written primarily for children ages nine to twelve. Also, I have to define words here and there so that kids can tell their parents these books are educational. By the way, kids, *patronizing*, as used here, means to talk down to someone or treat them as inferior. It can also refer to the act of being a customer (or *patron*) to a business. English is full of words with seemingly unrelated double or triple meanings. Bore, check, punch, right, pen, scale, tear, fair, cleave, and bolt are just a few examples. More on this later.

apparently this barbaric death trap is the usual form of punishment for something like that. On top of that, you don't seem all that frightened to be here, more like excited. So either you're insane, or you meant to be here."

The boy clapped softly. "Very nice. You're smarter than you look." He reached into his hair and slowly unwound what looked like a length of golden thread. "Suregold," he explained. "Usually they feed the slaves to sciferats on Thursdays, but apparently they broke their pattern."

"How rude. And how are you with humdrungelobs?"

"Well," he said, rubbing his chin, "they're *much* harder to kill. My plan was to *not* do this on a humdrungelob day."

"What do you plan to gain from all this?" I asked. The humdrungelob was getting close now, and we began edging away. Fierce as it was, the thing obviously couldn't see or hear very well.

"I want to be a slave."

"That's nice. You can be *my* slave, if you want. Or are you looking for a particular master?"

He flashed a grin. "You guessed it. The wizard Broca has been slave shopping the last couple Thursdays, and I want to be his apprentice." Tav picked up a rock and threw it. The humdrungelob lunged toward the place where it fell, and we began walking in the opposite direction.

"I don't get it," I said. "He wants an apprentice or he wants a slave?"

Tav shrugged. "He's a bit…odd. But he's the most powerful wizard in Tarinea. If I can get him to take me in, it will all be worth it. My old master didn't really work out."

I nodded. "Well, Tav, you're sort of in luck. I happen to be an expert at defeating humdrungelobs."

He stopped short, giving me a suspicious look. "Really…"

"Oh, yeah," I said. "And by expert, I mean I read a book about it once, and I have a really stupid, highly dangerous plan."

He grinned. "Sounds good to me."

Of course, I had by now remembered what you, the careful reader, no doubt remembered several pages ago: Not long ago, Drake forced me to read a strange and boring book entitled *Hugging the Humdrungelob: Why the Infamous Beasts of Sayco Are Nothing to Fear* by Loquacious Bright. That little volume, by the way, not only gave a detailed description of the beasts (which is why it had seemed familiar to me earlier) but also an equally detailed—if disturbing—method for incapacitating one.[17]

"One condition," I said, holding up a finger. "If you get enslaved or apprenticed or whatever to this Broca guy out of this, you have to take me with you. I have some problems of my own, and I could use the help of a powerful wizard."

I was thinking, of course, of my situation in the tomb of Rone. Maybe this Broca guy, if he really was a powerful wizard, would have an idea of how I could get out of it

17 Of course, I knew Drake would never let me hear the end of it if he ever found out how helpful his reading assignment had been, so I made a silent vow not to tell him.

without getting anyone killed. It also occurred to me that since turning E6 on the turncoat generally brought me to a place where one of the lost bloodstones was located, there was a solid chance one was hiding in Tarinea. In which case, it might be wise to consult someone who was, no doubt, an expert on the city itself.

The boy considered my offer for a long minute—much longer than I had expected. Finally, he shrugged. "Whatever."

I held out my hand, and we shook.

"Good, then," I said. "We'll need a distraction, but I think I've got that covered. The hard part will be not getting eaten when I grab the tongue. Can you quack like a duck?"

He frowned. "Are you insane, Simon?"

"A little," I admitted. "Who isn't?"

I turned E1 and pushed my dumb clone out into the arena.

Of all the animals, man is the only one that is cruel. He is the only one that inflicts pain for the pleasure of doing it.

—Mark Twain[18]

Dumb Me stumbled forward, spotted the humdrungelob, and began waving excitedly at it. The humdrungelob snorted and charged, thundering toward us at incredible speed.

"Your distraction is about to be dead," Tav warned. "What do we do next?"

I turned D6 (*Lightning*) and managed to aim the bolt of lightning so that it struck the ground a couple feet from Dumb Me. As I'd hoped, that startled him enough to bolt[19] away, causing the humdrungelob to swerve in a

18 Real name: Samuel Langhorne Clemens. Author of *The Adventures of Tom Sawyer*. Fun fact: He was born with the appearance of Halley's Comet in 1835 and died the day after its next appearance in 1910, as he said he would. Halley's Comet, by the way, swings by earth every 75.32 years and will make its next appearance in 2061, which means that *you* (assuming you are currently under fifty) might be around to see it. Eat your vitamins!

19 As I mentioned earlier, the word *bolt* has several meanings. *Bolt* is a prime example of a homonym. Homonyms are words that *sound* alike, but don't mean the same thing. They may or may not be spelled

different direction.

"So you *are* a wizard," Tav said, looking mildly impressed.

"Hurry," I said, ignoring him. "Run after them. As soon as my dumb clone gets eaten, I want you to stand right in front of it and start quacking like a duck. If you could *look* like a duck, that would be even better."

"Seriously?"

"Seriously."

"So I get to go look like an idiot, and you get to what, kill it?"

"Yep."

"Arial Black!" Tav swore. "This better be enough to impress Broca. And you better not mess it up and get me eaten!"

With that, he smoothed his hair out. As he did, his skin turned yellow, his arms became slightly wingish,[20] and he sprouted little feathers from random places.

As I had hoped, Tav was a real wizard, if a fledgling[21] one.

I turned C1 (*Chameleon*) and mostly disappeared—

---

the same. In this example we have bolt (a unit of lightning), bolt (to run suddenly), bolt (a bundle of fabric), bolt (a threaded fastener), and bolt (a heavy crossbow arrow). All of these words are spelled the same and pronounced the same, but they have distinctly different meanings. By the way, there are several more forms of the word *bolt,* but I sensed that you were getting bored. Not to be confused with *board* (I would never compare you to a plank of wood) or *bored* (I hope you are not having a hole drilled through you right now).

20 Not a word.

21 (1) Young, immature, or underdeveloped. (2) A baby bird in the process of growing feathers. Clever, I know.

at which Tav gave an appreciative whistle—and we stepped out of the swirling dust cloud together. He ran off in pursuit of the rampaging humdrungelob, and I was right behind him. When we got close, I veered off to the right and began to circle around to take the beast from a different angle. Not for the first time, I was glad that I was mostly invisible, and that Rellik's boots made no sound whatsoever on the ground. I was kicking up a pretty good dust cloud and leaving footprints, but the humdrungelob didn't seem to notice those things.

The monster had corned[22] Dumb Me by now.

It reared back on its hind legs again, and Dumb Me pressed his back against the wall. The beast opened its huge mouth and extended a tubular purple tongue. It was at least twenty feet long and at least a foot in diameter, and it reminded me of a pool noodle that had been supersized and then came horribly to life.

In a last desperate effort, Dumb Me stuck his hands inside his fake turncoat and started turning knobs. Nothing happened, of course. The purple tongue seized him and reeled him in like a toad catching a fly.

"Noooo, I don't like this!" Dumb Me screamed, and then the monster's myriad pointy teeth engulfed him.

I was shocked that Dumb Me could speak. However, I felt somewhat comforted by the fact that he was smart

---

22 Sorry. I meant to say *cornered*. To corn meat means to cure it with large rock-sized pieces (corns) of salt. And while the humdrungelob did intend to eat Dumb Me, it didn't go through the trouble of corning him.

enough to know when he was being eaten.[23]

The humdrungelob belched again and dropped back to all fours, and I sneaked between its back legs, moving toward the front of its body. I looked up into its partially open maw and saw the monster's three tongues wrapped up inside. I knew from my reading that there would be three. A purple one for eating, a red one for fighting, and a yellow one, which it used to impress potential mates. It was the yellow tongue that was directly connected to the humdrungelob's heart. An *extended* yellow tongue, then, was the monster's biggest weakness, as the two-foot-thick rhino hide was very tough to penetrate, even with magical means.

Luckily, ducks made humdrungelobs absolutely love crazy.

"Now, Tav!" I shouted when I had moved to a safe distance again. The monster spun around at the sound of my voice and saw Tav standing there, waving his newly sprouted feathers. To Tav's credit, he really put on a show, quacking, waddling back and forth, and shaking his... well, you get the picture. A person has to have a lot of confidence (or no self-respect whatsoever) to act that way in public.

By the way, in case you are wondering what role ducks play in the humdrungelob mating ritual, they

---

23 By the way, for those of you disturbed by my nonchalant (and sometimes irreverent) disregard for the life of my dumb clone, let me assure you that he is not a real person or a living being of any sort. He is nothing more than a temporary, reproducible magical projection, devoid of any life or humanbeingness of his own. I think...

are something between chaperones and matchmakers. Needless to say, to a humdrungelob, the arrival of a duck means it's time to go into dating mode.

At the sight of the giant ducklike figure, the humdrungelob's eyes grew wide. It sat back on its hind legs and began to hum softly. Then, as I had hoped, it shot its huge yellow tube tongue out and began spinning it in a wide circle like a cowboy swinging a lasso overhead.

Pleased that my ridiculous plan was working and that Tav had not yet been eaten, I began to time the rotation of the tongue. The next part was going to be very dangerous, and I needed to get it right on the first try. According to Drake's book, when it comes to humdrungelob slaying, the alternative to duck-baiting involves three dozen torches of Midnight Blue flame and a freshly shaved caribou, and I just didn't have those kinds of resources.

When the tongue was in its proper point of rotation, I turned B1 (*Leap)*, B4 (*Ninja*), and, in hopes that doing so might help to soften the undoubtedly considerable blow that I was about to receive, C3 (*Sponge*). Then I leaped thirty feet in the air, adjusting my arc with ninjalike accuracy so that the giant yellow two-ton tongue slapped me right out of the air. I clung on to it for dear life, and to this day I cannot hug a tree (especially a wet one) without having disturbing flashbacks of that moment.

Before long, I felt a sudden warmth fill the tongue, which meant that the monster, thinking it had made contact with another humdrungelob (much like humans, humdrungelobs aren't too bright when they're in mating mode), had connected the tongue's blood flow directly with its heart and begun to fill it up in preparation for the next display in the mating ritual.

Feeling rather pleased with myself, I raised Kylanthus and spoke its name. Red fire erupted out of thin air and wrapped itself around the blade. I swung it with everything I had, and in a flash of crimson flame, I cut the tongue cleanly in two.

5 Slaves

The test of the morality of a society is what it does for its children.

—Dietrich Bonhoeffer[24]

Seeing as how this is a children's book, and therefore characteristically devoid of blood and violence, I am going to skip over the next minute or so of action. Suffice it to say, the humdrungelob died. As I stood there afterward, my sword covered in monster goo, a thunderous applause rolled down from above, and I was struck by just how many people must have been up there.

My chameleon invisibility effect was wearing off now, and no doubt the audience was surprised to see me alive and well after I (Dumb Me) had been eaten earlier. Likewise, Tav was molting his feathers and turning back to his normal color. Our onlookers were likely awed by his uncanny ability to quack like a duck and shuffle back and forth. Tav bowed grandly, and I couldn't help liking him a bit more for that. Too bad that I had just made him

24 A German theologian who resisted the Nazi Dictatorship of Adolf Hitler. He was imprisoned in a concentration camp, and later executed.

look like a fool in front of wizard what's-his-face that he was trying to impress. His chances of winning a cool tutor were probably gone, but at least we were still alive.

The applause died down to a dull roar, and in the center of the arena, a golden ring of light appeared on the dirt. We walked toward it. When we stepped inside, the ring lifted into the air, taking us with it. It was as if we were standing in an invisible elevator.

As we rose slowly upward, the people that I had heard cheering earlier came into view. They were seated in rows, not unlike a sports arena back home. Seated at regular intervals in the front row were King's Guards. They each held a golden staff, and from the end of each staff a bluish mist issued, so that the streams came together and filled the air above the arena with a semitransparent cloud.

Later, I would learn that this cloud prevented wizards from using magic to escape. It was also suddenly apparent to me why this arena was called the Maw: There above the topmost benches, great toothlike projections jutted out from the arena's stone walls. If you closed one eye and looked straight up at the starry night sky obscured by those toothy stones, it wasn't hard to imagine that the arena itself was inside the open mouth of some enormous beast.

I was looking up like that when Tav slapped me as our invisible platform came to a halt. "Check it out!" he hissed from beside me. "It's *Hiamene*."

I wasn't sure who Hiamene was, but there was a cute teenage girl in front of us now. She sat between a group of older wizards at the center of a curved table of sparkling black marble suspended above the center of the arena. She had dark, luxurious skin, and there were beads of gold and precious gems glinting in her braided hair. She wore an intricate yellow dress that put me in mind of a Japanese kimono, and she had dreamy eyes.[25]

She raised a golden fan to her mouth and spoke into it, and her voice was magically magnified so that it boomed around the arena, forcing silence from the crowd.

"Congratulations, slave children. By your valor, you have won a second chance at life. Behold the buyers!"

At these words, a line of people walked down from one of the front-row benches and moved to stand on the invisible floor.

"Inspect them at your will," Hiamene said, her voice no longer magnified.

The weird pack of wizards swarmed us like ducks around a breadcrumb, and I was overwhelmed by strange faces and accents. There was a woman with a stuffed lemur on her hat; a man in robes of liquid gold, bedecked in jewelry; a boy no older than ourselves who spoke like an uppity bank investor; an old man with a stooped back; and several other characters. Some asked us questions—What's your name? How old are you? What magic can you do? How many eggs can you eat without throwing up?—while others had more unique means of inspecting us.

---

25 Of course, when you're thirteen, *every* girl that looks at you has dreamy eyes.

The boy asked to see our fingernails. The woman with the lemur hat tapped a little silver file against our teeth, listening carefully. Strangest of all was the man with the stooped back. First of all, his back itself was weirdly pronounced, more like a sharpened hump. He stared down constantly and would not meet our eyes, and there was a strange object that floated by his shoulder at all times. It was unlike anything I'd ever seen before but reminded me vaguely of a large black button because it was round and had four holes near the center like a button does. He waited to go last, and when the others were satisfied with their inspections, he took a large silver ring out of his pocket and placed it on his index finger. Then, with the same hand, he slapped me right in the face.

"Ouch!" I said. "Child abuse!"

But the man was watching his hand with interest. A second later, his hand turned blue, and his palm began to pulse with light.

He slapped Tav in the face next, and his hand turned black. After that, he nodded and stepped away.

"Commence the bidding," Hiamene said again, her voice carrying all around the Maw.

One of the older wizards beside her stood and began the bidding.

"The older one first. Do I hear five robels? Five to Lord Helnca," he said, nodding to a stubby wizard on the left. "Do I hear seven? Seven, to Lady Crozwhile." The lady in the lemur hat winked at me. "Who will go ten? You, sir? You?" The man in gold robes bid ten, and then he and the lemur lady went all the way up to twenty-five, with her ending up on top.

"Sold to Lady Crozwhile. Now I begin the bidding on the one that can turn into a duck. Do I hear ten?"

The old man with the hump clapped his hands loudly above his head.

"Yes, Lord Broca?" the auctioneer said, pausing his spiel.

The floating button thing beside the stooped man spit out a little sheet of lavender paper, like a receipt, and Lady Crozwhile tore it off and read it:

"I will pay two hundred robels for the pair."

There was a gasp from the audience.

"Sold!" the auctioneer squeaked and banged his fist on the marble table.

"But you already sold one to me!" the lady in the hat complained.

It didn't seem to matter. A member of the King's Guard came and escorted the losing bidders away.

When they were gone, Hiamene rose to her feet. "I hereby pronounce the games closed!" she boomed. "Tomorrow, watch a pair of twin sisters get fed to a gorgon!"

The audience cheered and began to disperse.

Hiamene slumped back into her seat, her earlier dignity and grace forgotten. She looked at me as I walked past, following the stooped man toward the exit. "Good luck," she mouthed, but her expression said something else. It was the sort of expression you wear when you dump a mostly dead fish in the toilet or open a gift to find a hand-knitted suit from Great Aunt Sandy on Christmas morning:[26] part horror, part resignation. Very, very little hope.

We followed Broca and his bobbing button butler into the stands, down the ramps, and onto a starlit cobblestone street. We followed him as he ambled slowly across the city. He soon grew tired, and he began to grunt with every other step, his breaths coming hard. Never at any point did he speak to us or make eye contact.

Eventually there was a shift in our surroundings as we passed into a different quarter of the city. Stone houses and fences gave way to the pipes and wheels and steel slab walls of industrial buildings. We turned down a side street, and the road rose. Above us, at the end of a dark lane, stood a dilapidated factory with off-kilter walls. As we neared its outer gates, I saw glowing barbed wire coiled along the tops of the walls and fences that surrounded the place. One of the floating button thing's holes flashed, and the gate slid open with a demonic squeal.

We passed into a courtyard-type space, and I gazed up at a maze of rusted catwalks, ladders, stairs, chutes, pulleys, and buckets. A barred door opened beside us, startling me, and the old man ushered us inside. Then he shut the door behind us, locking us in our room.

Or should I say, our cell.

---

26 This never happened to me. I don't know what would give you that sort of idea. Nor did I wear it for photographic evidence to be procured. Let's forget I ever mentioned such a ridiculously specific analogy.

The button ball spit out another sheet of paper, and Broca ripped it off and passed it through the bars to me. Then he turned and walked painfully away, the black orb bobbing in the air beside his shoulder, until he was gone into the shadows.

I looked down and read the paper out loud. The ink was red:

SLEEP NOW.
FOOD TOMORROW.
MUCH TO DISCUSS.
WELCOME HOME.

"Huh," I said.

"What?"

"He let me keep Kylanthus."

"Ky—"

"Sorry. My sword. He let me keep my sword."

"Is that really the name of your sword?" Tav said. He was bending over to inspect the hilt.

"Sure. Why?"

His brow furrowed. "No reason."

"I'm just saying, I thought he would take it away or something. You know?"

"Broca is a very powerful wizard, Simon. He's probably not worried about you having a sword. He let me keep my dagger." He indicated the knife on his belt.

I shrugged, looking around our cell. "Well?" I said, "you got what you wanted. Is it everything you dreamed of?"

Tav sat down on the damp metal floor. He laced his

hands behind his head and lay down, grinning as if he had just won the lottery.

"Simon, you just wait. It's going to be great. Absolutely great."

6 TO KILL A MONSTER

I have no use for adventures. Nasty disturbing uncomfortable things! Make you late for dinner!

—Bilbo Baggins[27]

Just to recap: So far I've been arrested, imprisoned, tortured, fed to a monster, and sold into slavery. I've also *slain* said monster, made a new frenemy, and procured another sketchy wizard teacher/slave master. And all that before chapter eight! As you can see, we're on track to make this another slow, boring volume of my biography.[28]

27 An "'Excitable little fellow,' said Gandalf… 'Gets funny queer fits, but he is one of the best—as fierce as a dragon in a pinch.'" —J.R.R. Tolkien.

28 This, of course, is sarcasm. *Sarcasm* is the noble art of using irony (or saying the opposite of what you mean) to mock or show contempt. Sarcasm can be a good icebreaker, and it's a decent source of laughs among friends. Sometimes you can use sarcasm on strangers, and it will seem like you are speaking the same secret language, so you begin feeling like you know each other better than you really do. Sarcasm's main purpose is to allow you to be rude in a socially acceptable manner. As such, it is not used by people with class or dignity. As careful readers will have noticed, *I* use it incessantly. In fact, large portions of this autobiography are written in it. Sarcasm is also a decent way to peg yourself as someone of mediocre intelligence, offend those closest to you, and create a palpable cloud of bad vibes around yourself (just read the negative reviews of this

Tav was like a wild, starving wolf.

When his smile eventually faded, he just sat there, outwardly calm, eyes wide yet alight with fear and anticipation. After a while, I fell asleep for what I guessed was a couple hours. All that monster slaying and torture had worn me out. When I woke, he was still sitting like that. Thinking of who knows what.

When I finally got him talking, he told me what he knew about Broca. How he was a social outcast. How the other wizards of Tarinea mocked his theories and spurned his company. For all that, they couldn't deny that he was a genius. He had come to Tarinea ten years ago and been unpopular ever since, but his work on subterraneous biparticle vapor accumulations (whatever that was) had actually saved the city from destruction, and it was hardly polite to banish a local hero. He could neither speak nor hear without the help of his biopod, Sipher. He was a cripple too, though *how* he got his limp and his weirdly stooped back was apparently a matter of some debate.

"Most people believe that he got on the wrong side of a Harskavian mudmonkey. Don't ask me why. *I* think one of his experiments went wrong, but my father..."

"What does your father think?" I prompted when he didn't continue. Tav was turning out to be a wealth of knowledge, and I didn't want him to clam[29] up.

---

book). So, use it at your own risk. DISCLAIMER: If you have ever voluntarily swallowed a Tide pod, you might not have the common sense necessary to wield sarcasm responsibly. In fact, you might not have the sense God gave a gym sock. Sorry. :(

29 Clams, being the deep-sea dwelling invertebrate mollusks they

Tav frowned. "How long do you think he is going to leave us in here?"

"The real question is, how will he react to our breaking out?" I breathed into my cupped hands to warm them, then turned A3 (*Curse*), and kicked down the door.

It splintered from its hinges and clattered to the floor.

"Hmm," Tav said, nonplussed. "Let's go find out."

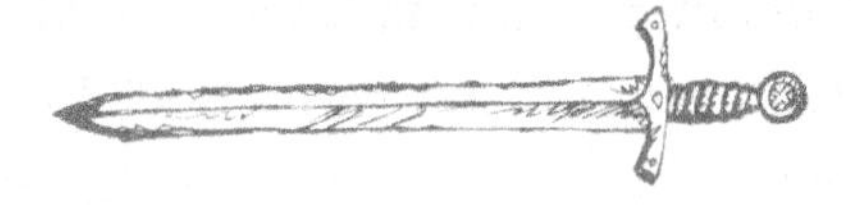

The old factory at Doverock (which Tav tells me is the name of this place) once made, well, *doverock*—the beautiful white stone out of which much of the city of Tarinea was built. It was a magically enhanced substance, apparently, and the old factory bore witness to this with a litany of scarred walls, burned floors, mangled heaps of metal and stone, and, last but not least, the fifty-foot crater that sat where the factory's main stonecutting bath once stood.

Apparently this last incident caused the original owners to completely rebuild somewhere else. That was all very long ago, of course. Now the place was full of sealed-off hallways, doors half rusted shut, and small, nameless creatures living inside of places that normal occupants would never have stood for. Like a family of foxes with its den in an old sink. A bird's nest in the linkage of a door.

We found Broca inside what was clearly the original

---

are, don't say much. In fact, on the Don'tsaymuch scale (http://austinjbailey.com/dontsaymuch-scale/), they are listed just above rocks. Hence, they are the subject of descriptive phrases like this.

chemistry lab. The ceiling and half of one wall had long since been blown away in an explosion, but whether it had been by Broca or the previous occupants was unclear. Beneath a red sunrise, Broca stood in the center of a huge cluster of bubbling, steaming, gurgling flasks, tubes, beakers, and crucibles. The floor was sunken so that he stood far below us, with several rickety iron staircases between us and him. He was dressed in the same dark nondescript attire he had been in previously, except that he now wore a green-hilted smallsword at his side.

He held up his hands when he saw us, and we stopped. Sipher zoomed toward us, printing out a roll of receipt paper as he came:

TOOK YOU LONG ENOUGH.
COME DOWN CAREFULLY.
DON'T TOUCH THE NEGATIZED ACRIMON.

"The what?" I said.

"Not sure," Tav muttered, looking around cautiously.

Sipher printed again.

THE BUBBLY, GLOWING RED STUFF ON THE RIGHT.

"Ah, yes. Of course."

As we descended, we were careful to give the simmering vat of red goo a wide berth. It looked safely contained in the tall steel canister (the biggest thing in the room), but I think we would have avoided it even without instructions to do so—it smelled like roadkill.

When we reached the old wizard, he smiled at us. Or at least, I think he did. He had a face like a gopher rockfish, with a frown so deeply set that even his smiles turned down. His hair was barely there at all, but his eyes were young and clever.

Sipher rotated ninety degrees, and a light flashed from one of his button holes, which was apparently some form of communication, though it meant nothing to me. He printed again:

START WITH YOUR QUESTIONS.

"I take it we don't actually have to sleep in a cell?" I said.

"Why did you pick both of us?" Tav said. "Wizards only have one apprentice at a time."

Sipher printed again. Each time he did, the previous bit of lavender paper fell away and disintegrated in a puff of dust.

I BOUGHT BOTH OF YOU, BUT I WILL ONLY CHOOSE ONE OF YOU TO BE MY APPRENTICE. YOU ARE RIGHT IN YOUR ASSESSMENT: HISTORY HAS TAUGHT US ONE PUPIL AT A TIME IS QUITE ENOUGH TO HANDLE.

"But how will you pick?" Tav said, shouldering me aside slightly.

Broca raised an eyebrow as Sipher printed. Tav tore the paper off eagerly, read it, and handed it to me.

I WILL CHOOSE THE ONE WHO SURVIVES.

"Survives what?" I asked.

YOUR QUEST. DON'T YOU KNOW THAT EVERY GREAT WIZARD STORY BEGINS WITH A QUEST?

"And what is this quest?"

He turned his back to us, but Sipher kept printing.

TO KILL A MONSTER.

"Oy," I said, deflating. "Another one?"

NOTHING LIKE THAT PLAYTHING YOU DESTROYED YESTERDAY. A REAL MONSTER. A THING TRULY TO BE FEARED. A THING THAT I MYSELF HAVE BEEN UNABLE TO BEST THESE LONG YEARS.

I glanced sideways at Tav, who looked as skeptical as I felt. How were *we* supposed to defeat something that was too powerful for Broca?

"What is this beast we're supposed to kill?" Tav said.

Broca turned back to us and gave Tav a searching look.

I WILL SHOW YOU. BUT LATER. SHOWING IS ALWAYS BETTER THAN TELLING, DON'T YOU AGREE?

"Wait. You have this thing?" Tav said excitedly. "You have it here?"

I HAVE HAD IT FOR MANY YEARS NOW. FINDING IT WAS SUPPOSED TO BE THE HARDEST PART. LITTLE DID I KNOW...

"Let's go and kill it now, then!" Tav said. "We're ready."

"Uh… I'm not ready," I pointed out. "I prefer to look first, research second, and fight maybe not at all."

Tav glared at me.

Sipher printed.

GOOD. HUMOR WILL SERVE YOU WELL. YOU WILL NEED IT.

He tucked his thumbs into his belt and spread his legs a bit, settling into a strong stance. I realized that despite his hump and his gimp leg, this old codger had some fight left in him.

NOW WE KNOW WHY I BROUGHT YOU HERE.
WHY DID YOU COME?

We didn't say anything. I, for one, wasn't in the mood to spill my deepest thoughts to a sketchy stranger just yet.

Broca poked Tav in the chest, and Sipher began printing somewhat furiously.

IT DOESN'T MATTER. I KNOW ANYWAY. YOU ARE HERE BECAUSE YOU LUST FOR POWER. POWER AND MORE POWER, WHEREVER YOU CAN GET IT THE QUICKEST. THIS IS GOOD, BUT IT IS ALSO BAD. YOU ARE RIGHT TO THINK THAT I CAN HELP YOU FIND IT. YOU HAVE BROUGHT TROUBLE TO ME, HOWEVER. YOUR FATHER WILL NOT LIKE THIS ARRANGEMENT.

He turned to me.

YOU HAVE TWO PROBLEMS. FIRST, THERE APPEARS TO BE SOMETHING WRONG WITH YOUR MAGIC. OBVIOUSLY YOU CANNOT ACCESS IT DIRECTLY, AND YOU ARE STUCK CHANNELING IT THROUGH…THIS.

He ran an exploratory hand along the sleeve of my turncoat, and I recoiled at his percipience.[30]

BUT THAT'S NOT ALL, IS IT? THERE IS SOMETHING DEEPER, SOME CORE CONTAMINATION OF YOUR POWER. FASCINATING…

30 Skill in perceiving.

YOUR OTHER PROBLEM IS A QUESTION, I TAKE IT. IT HANGS ABOUT YOU LIKE A NOOSE. BOTH OF THESE THINGS I CAN HELP YOU WITH, SIMON.

He took a step back and considered us together.

I CAN HELP YOU BOTH, BUT I WILL ONLY HELP ONE OF YOU. THE ONE WHO WINS, OF COURSE.

"The first one to kill the monster?" I guessed.

"Or the last one alive?" Tav put in, looking at me darkly.

Broca held up his hands.

YOU DECIDE.

"And if we lose?" I said. "And live, I mean."

He pointed at the vat of deadly red stuff.

I wasn't sure exactly what that meant, but I decided right then and there to never find out. I decided I didn't care much about winning this so-called contest, either. This Broca guy was bad news. Forget about whether he could help me. There were bound to be other smart wizards in Tarinea who I could seek out. I was out of there.

Just then, Broca held out his hands, one to each of us. In each palm lay a gray iron coin with an engraved symbol that I didn't recognize.

THESE ARE FOR YOU.

The coins leaped from his hands before we could even reach out to take them. They zoomed toward our heads. Mine struck me square in the forehead, and I staggered backward.

"Gah!" Tav said. "What is this thing?"

The coin was still stuck to my forehead, and when I reached up to grab it, I found it embedded there, sunk into the skin.

Broca twisted his hand, and a third coin appeared in it. This one he threw into the air so that it passed beyond where the ceiling had once been. The coin exploded in midair, creating a fireball six feet across.

We stared at Broca, dumbfounded, and Sipher printed again.

THESE COINS ARE A LITTLE THING OF MY OWN INVENTION. YOU CAN THINK OF THEM AS... INSURANCE. COME AND GO AS YOU WISH. GO ANYWHERE YOU LIKE THROUGHOUT THE CITY, BUT DON'T TRY TO LEAVE OR GET OUT OF PLAYING MY LITTLE GAME.
DO YOU UNDERSTAND?

Tav nodded.

"YOU MAD OLD CODGER!" I shouted. "I'd rather go back to the Maw than dance around like your little puppet!" I drew Kylanthus and breathed its name, igniting the blade in red flames.[31]

Broca took a step back but smiled at me. He drew his own sword, a thin, delicate thing, and raised it in invitation.

Not quite sure what to do next, and very aware that at any moment my head might get smashed in by a six-foot-diameter fireball, I reached into the turncoat and turned a new knob, A7, hoping for a miracle.

---

31 There are actually two possible explanations for my little outburst

No sooner had I turned the knob than I had a stroke of brilliance the likes of which even *I* wasn't used to. I saw my way out. Rather, I saw that I *had* no way out, but I also saw that there were several things I could do to improve my situation. Sometimes when you start down a path, the best thing to do is see it through with gusto.

I turned B4 (*Ninja*), D1 (*Copy*), D2, and D6 (*Lightning*). A sheep fell from the sky, and Broca caught it with one arm, looking shocked. I spun around, weaving Kylanthus through the air with expert precision, forcing Broca back another step. I struck his sword, and it fell to the ground. I lunged to retrieve his blade, and he twisted, kicking it away. Of course, *before* he kicked it away, I did something very sneaky, which I will tell you about later. At the same moment, lightning streaked out of the clear sky and struck—as I knew it would—the biggest thing in the room: the tall steel drum of Negatized Acrimon.

An explosion the likes of which was generally reserved for mining crews and war zones lit the lab, knocking me clean off my feet and sending Tav and Broca staggering back. Burbling waves of flaming lava rose out of the tank and engulfed the whole right side of the room in seconds.

Broca, who was still holding the sheep, tossed it away,

---

here. You will have to decide for yourself which is true: One is that I suddenly felt as though I had lost all control of the situation. A tough thing to swallow just then, since I had come to Tarinea trying to escape *another* situation in which I was powerless. The other explanation is that I *hate* coin collecting. Therefore, when I found myself being forced, against my will, to not only collect a coin, but display it on my face, I completely lost my cool.

unfortunately toward the Negatized Acrimon Lightning Lava.[32] He raised both hands high above his head, and though he spoke no booming spell, there was a flash of blue light. It started above his hands and radiated outward like a ripple in a moonlit pond until it had touched everything in the lab. When it rolled over me, I felt instantly at peace. Likewise, the lava simmered away into water and steam, the fires went out, and the smoke rolled off into the cheerful sky.

Unfortunately, the effects of this impressive "chill out" spell did not extend to Broca himself, who turned on me, positively livid.

Realizing in that moment that I probably didn't actually stand a chance against him, I sheathed Kylanthus and tried to look as innocent as possible.

But he wasn't having it. He was trembling with fury, and for a moment I felt bad that he couldn't scream or curse like a normal person (Sipher was floating several feet away printing out sheet after sheet of blank paper). He raised one finger, and I flew into the air as though shot by a cannon. I struck the steel wall of the lab and dangled there, fifteen feet in the air. The coin embedded in my forehead went white hot, and I cried out just before I lost consciousness.

---

32 No sheep were harmed in the making of this book. Except that one, obviously.

7 THE GROAN

Monsters are real, and ghosts are real too. They live inside us, and sometimes, they win.

—Stephen King[33]

"What were you thinking?"

That was the first thing that I heard when I came to. We were back in our "cell," though the door was wide open. Despite a raging headache, I wasn't surprised to be still alive, and I was feeling quite pleased with myself.

Tav didn't look very impressed.

"I say again. What were you thinking? He could have killed you! He could have killed me!"

I groaned, putting a hand to my head and noticing the coin was still embedded there. It took some effort to get to my feet. "Nah. He wasn't going to kill us. Trust me, this will be good for us."

Tav frowned. "Funny you should say that…"

"Funny?"

33 A brilliant writer of what are often strange and horrifying books. He writes faster than some people can read and better than most people can appreciate.

"Yeah. He… Broca actually laughed after he, you know…"

"Almost killed me?"

"Yeah. He just threw back his head and laughed."

"Strange that he can laugh but he can't speak," I noted.

"Uh. Strange that you destroyed his lab and he laughed about it, I say."

I waved a hand as if it was the simplest thing in the world. The truth was, when I turned that new knob, A7, I had such a brainwave that I knew exactly what to do to impress Broca, make him trust me, and get a tactical advantage against him at the same time. "Tav," I said, "sorry about that. The truth is, I needed a bit of a distraction in order to gain a tactical advantage."

"What do you mean, tactical advantage?" Tav said.

I reached into my turncoat and pressed E8 (*Stash*). Broca's thin sword appeared in midair, and I caught it.

Tav's jaw dropped open. "That's Broca's channeling vessel! How did you get it from him? Wait. He was holding it when we left…"

I grinned. Of course, I had turned D1 (*Copy*), and E8 (*Stash*) right after ninja-me knocked it out of his hand. The sword he then kicked out of my reach and recovered wasn't the *real* sword at all. This is, of course, the sneaky thing I mentioned earlier.

"I copied it," I said simply. "He has the fake. It's basically his magic wand, right?"

Tav rolled his eyes. "Right. People haven't used twigs as channeling vessels in a couple centuries, but whatever.

He's going to notice, you know. Maybe not for a while, though. Broca's a powerful wizard, and he doesn't need a channeling vessel for day-to-day stuff. It's more of a luxury. Still, he *will* notice. What are you going to do then?"

I studied the thin sword. It had a delicate curved hilt and a thin, tapered blade. It was very light, certainly under a pound. "I don't suppose we can use this against him?" I said hopefully.

Tav shook his head. "A channeling vessel only works for the person it's bonded to. Everyone knows that."

I cleared my throat. "They don't really use those as much where I'm from. Anyway, as for what to do when he discovers it's missing, I don't think it's going to be a problem. He's ruthless. As wizards go, I bet he's on the darker side of things. True? You know this, I guess. That's why you want to apprentice with him, seeing as how you're not exactly an angel yourself."

Tav folded his arms. "So?"

"So, how do you impress a *ruthless* potential master?"

Tav was seeing the light now, I could tell. "You do something horrible," he said.

"Right. You blow up his lab. You steal his magical sword vessel doohickey. You saw how powerful he is. I bet he can fix that lab or build a new one in about five minutes. Maybe. What he'll remember is how crazy and dangerous we are. And he'll like that." I winked at him.

Tav glowered. "How crazy and dangerous *you* are, you mean. I just stood there."

I shrugged.

"So you've realized it too," he said, and he began to circle me thoughtfully, hands clenched into fists, like someone about to pick a fight.

"Realized what?" I said, wondering what I had missed.

"He expects one of us to kill the other."

"WHAT?" I went over what he had said again. "No, I don't think he meant… Well…" I guess I *could* see that possibility. I wasn't sure what bothered me more: that Broca may have meant that or that Tav had jumped right to that conclusion.

"Only one of us can win," Tav was saying. "And you can bet it's going to be me." He stopped circling me then, and he had the look of someone who had just built up the courage to squish a spider.

"Whoa, just wait a minute!" I said. "I don't think it's time for us to start offing each other just yet! What *is* it with you people always turning on each other? This is exactly why the Sith became extinct."

"The what?"

"Never mind. I'm just saying, we don't know for *sure* yet if one of us has to die, right?"

He tilted his head in acquiescence.

"And we don't know for sure what we are facing yet, right? It might be something so crazy that our only chance of defeating it is to work together."

He unclenched his fists. "Yeah. I guess."

I breathed a sigh of relief. "Good. See? If you change your mind, you can always wait till after we defeat the monster, and *then* murder me." I held out my hand.

He considered me for a moment, then grinned. He shook my hand. "Deal."

Just then, Sipher came floating in through the open doorway. I hurriedly turned E8, and Broca's sword vanished into the turncoat.

"Geez, Sipher," I said. "Don't you knock?"

AS SOON AS THE RASH ONE WAKES UP, MEET ME IN THE LAB. THE TIME HAS COME FOR YOU TO BE ACQUAINTED WITH YOUR MONSTER.

Tav and I glanced at each other. "You ready?" he said.

"Duh. I was born ready."

We followed Sipher out in silence. No doubt Tav had a lot on his mind. I know I did. I was pretty sure I would be able to kill whatever monster Broca had locked in his basement, but what was I going to do about Tav? I needed Broca's help. Even if he couldn't give me a way out of my situation in Rone's tomb, it sounded like he could help decipher the mystery of the turncoat and what it was doing to my magic.

Then again, I wasn't about to kill Tav. I thought briefly about capturing Tav and locking him in the turncoat for a while. Letting Broca *think* he was dead. At the thought of it, my ears began to itch in earnest.

Okay, okay, I thought. *I wasn't seriously considering it.*

The itching did not go away, and I was put in mind of my friends again, stuck in one frozen moment, waiting for me to return and let one of them die. I felt guilty then, just a little bit, for abandoning them. I was sure of one thing: I couldn't do that again. Even if Tav had it in for me, I had to do my best to help him.

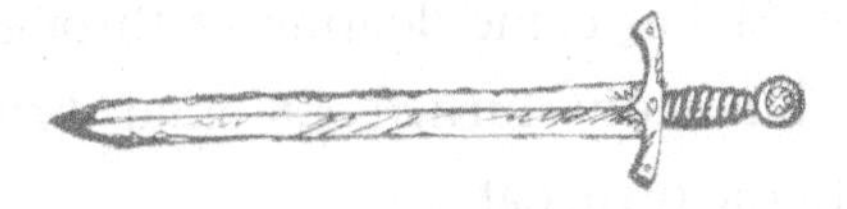

As my turncoat-augmented brilliant mind had predicted, Broca wasn't mad at all. He didn't even pretend to be, which was refreshing. The lab, of course, was good as new, though I noticed that a certain barrel in the corner had substantially less boiling red death-goo in it.

At the exact center of the lab, standing on the rug I had noticed earlier, Broca was holding a pair of strange-looking goggles. When we approached, he flicked a finger, and the rug rolled up and flew away, depositing itself in the corner.

Beneath it, in classic secretwizardy[34] fashion, was a reddish-black trapdoor[35] with a giant black padlock on it.

I was waiting for Broca to say something, to open the trapdoor, maybe, but nothing happened. "Wait a minute," I said. "Where did Sipher go?"

Tav and I glanced around. Neither of us could remember the moment that Sipher had left, but he certainly wasn't here anymore.

"Maybe he went to answer the door or something," Tav suggested.

We stared at Broca, and he stared back at us for a

34 This is a real word, and should not to be confused with secretpiratey, secretvillainy, or secretlittlesisterly, which are related (though totally different) expressions.
35 Yikes. Bloodstains, anyone?

while, then looked at the trapdoor, waiting.

"Well," I mumbled under my breath. "This is awkward."

"You don't have to mumble," Tav pointed out. "He can't hear us."

"You sure?"

"Sure," he said. "Everyone knows Broca's deaf as a doorknob."

"You think the monster is under that trapdoor?" I said.

"Obviously."

We stood in silence for a minute, and I found myself praying for Sipher's return. This was getting ridiculous.

I studied Broca out of the corner of my eye. He didn't look like much, really. Obviously he was powerful, but… "Tav, you sure this guy is worth all this trouble we're going through?"

"Definitely," Tav said. "If nothing else, my grandfather *hates* him, and my grandfather only hates people who are smarter than him and disagree with him at the same time. Not a long list. He's exactly the kind of master I want."

"If you say so," I said, eyeing Broca's boots. They were a strange pink color. "His boots look girly, though. Just saying. What kind of leather is pink?"

Tav grinned. "They probably came from a dragon or something."

"They *probably* came from a baby possum or something," I said.

Tav snorted with laughter.

Just then, we were spared further speculation by the

reappearance of Sipher. Broca glanced up from the bit of floor he had been staring at and glared at the little orb with disapproval, but it hovered over to us as if unaware.

THIS DOOR IS TO REMAIN LOCKED AT ALL TIMES, SIPHER PRINTED. EXCEPT WHEN ENTERING AND EXITING. IF YOU GO IN, LOCK IT BEHIND YOU. YOUR DEATH IS A SMALL PRICE TO PAY FOR KEEPING THE MONSTER SECURE.

"Cool," I said. "Do we get the combination?"

THE LOCK OPENS IN RECOGNITION OF MY MAGIC. THE COINS IN YOUR HEADS WILL SERVE THIS PURPOSE FOR YOU.

He gave us a long, penetrating stare.

IF YOU LET THE BEAST ESCAPE, EVEN IF IT IS AN ACCIDENT, I WILL HUNT YOU DOWN LIKE ANIMALS AND FEED YOUR EYES TO A CAT. DO YOU UNDERSTAND?

"I understand," Tav said.

"Eww," I said. "That's gross."

Broca flicked his finger again, and the trapdoor swung up, revealing a vertical tube, not unlike a sewer entrance. Speaking of sewers, the smell nearly knocked me unconscious yet again. Tav coughed, pulled a handkerchief out of his pocket, and tied it around his face.

Then we heard it: a deep groaning sound, like an angry landslide or a boat tearing in half underwater.

Broca didn't seem to notice. He stepped off the edge and floated downward into the tube. Assuming it was something akin to an indoor skydiving tunnel, I casually stepped over the edge as well.

I fell ten feet, screamed, and caught myself on a ladder hanging from the side of the wall.

"Nice," Tav said, sticking his head over the opening above. *He* came down the ladder.

When we reached the bottom, I was surprised to find not a leaky dungeon or a series of labyrinthine tunnels, but a single room. It was large—large enough to drop a two-story house inside—and stark white, lit by a single bright light from somewhere above.

The room was sterile and nearly empty. In the very center of it, chained to a golden eyebolt in the floor, was what looked like a small round box. It was made of brass, or gold maybe, and it had intricate decorations on the sides.

We heard the groaning sound again, loud enough to shake the ground. The round box shook too, as if it wanted to rattle free from its chain.

"What *is* that?" Tav asked.

A PRISON OF MY OWN DEVISING.
I CALL IT A GROAN.

"I can see why," I muttered.

To my surprise, Broca stepped right up to the box. He held out a hand, his fingers curved in a half circle, and a second later, he was holding a long staff. It was made of light and fire and shaped like a great snake wrapped around a gnarled tree branch. He tapped the lid off the Groan, and it popped open. As soon as it did, he was pointing the staff into the hole. The groaning turned into a roar, and it was so loud my teeth rattled. Broca hopped once more into the air above the hole, and then, incredibly, he fell into the little opening, shrinking right before our eyes.

"Like freaking Mary Poppins," I muttered, thinking of a similar stunt involving sidewalk chalk.

"What?" Tav said.

"I said stop shrieking and get hoppin'!"

"You did not," he said. "And I wasn't shrieking. *You* shrieked, or squeaked, or something, when you fell down that ladder."

"I do *not* squeak," I assured him. "Well, anyway, go on in. Go on. I'm right behind you."

He Mary Poppinsed[36] into the box as well, and I briefly considered snapping the lid shut and hightailing it out of there. But no doubt Broca could get out of his own prison box. And then there was the bigger issue: I *had* to know what was inside now.

You understand.

---

36 Not a word.

You always find something in the last place you look for it.
—Colonel Mark E. Bowen, USAF.[37]

I landed in outer space.

I know. Not what I expected either…

Or maybe I should say I landed on a giant circular slab of polished white marble suspended in the *midst* of space. The strange floor was about a football field in length and so white that it almost glowed. Stars swirled around us, above us, below us, like the newborn contents of some heavenly sneeze.

In the center of the white disc was a gold eyebolt like in the room above. And there, chained to the hook, was a…

…a…

…a…

---

37 I'd tell you who he is, but it's classified.

…baby zebra!!!

I'm kidding, of course…

It was a little girl.

She was maybe four years old, and she was curled up in a little ball, fast asleep.

"What the..." Tav said.

"HEY," I said, brushing past Broca and rolling up my sleeves. "You're keeping a little kid in here? What's the big idea?"

I was intent on setting the girl free at once, but Broca grabbed the neck of the turncoat and brought me to a halt. Sipher, who must have followed us down the ladder, swung around in front of me and printed a short note.

STEP BACK VERY SLOWLY.

NOW.

IT IS NOT SAFE TO WAKE HER UP IN THIS ROOM.

Feeling a shred of doubt, I complied.

Sipher was printing again.

THE BEAST IS TREACHEROUS. LOOK.

Broca handed us each a pair of those strange goggles he had been holding. I put them on, and then stifled a squeak.[38] The white disc upon which we stood was covered almost completely by the massive scaled body of what was unmistakably a blue-and-purple-and-white dragon. Green-and-golden wings, which were two or three school

38 Dang it. I guess I *do* squeak. There comes a day in every man's life when he realizes that—only occasionally, mind you, but *more* often if he is a real-life monster-fighting wizard hero—he squeaks. There also comes a day when he realizes that he will never play professional baseball. Both of these days are very sad. Sniff. Don't look at me right now...

buses long, were nestled beside a spiky violet head. The dragon groaned, or rather, snored, again, and from this close, it was an overpowering and disturbing noise, ripe with discontent and malice.

The white disc shook violently, bringing me to my knees. Luminescent smoke curled out of yard-high nostrils.

I am not ashamed to say that I was suddenly quite afraid. Not because of how big or scary looking or firebreathey[39] the thing obviously was… Okay, partially because of that. What frightened me most was its anger. I had never seen anything—*anyone* so angry in their sleep. I prayed right then and there that it would never wake up.

Sipher printed.

I WILL NOW WAKE THE BEAST UP. STAND BEHIND ME.

Figures…

Broca stepped forward and raised his fiery staff. He slammed it down hard against the floor, and it made a loud crack.

The dragon's eyes snapped open, revealing dark star-shaped pupils in a sea of electric blue. The eyes met mine, and I felt a white-hot fire sear my mind, burning up all thought.

Broca's staff flashed, and the pain vanished, my thoughts tumbling back into form.

The dragon rose to its feet, smoke billowing down as it towered over us.

---

39 You decide.

While Tav and I prepared to die, Broca calmly raised a hand, reaching up as if to grab something that only he could see. He wrapped his hand around an invisible something in midair and then whipped it downward. As he did, the whole world around us was peeled aside. It was as if he had torn away the canvas of a painting to reveal something entirely different underneath.

The dragon was still there, as we were, but the slab of white marble upon which we stood now rested at the bottom of a tranquil valley. Green, moss-covered, rocky mountains rose upward on all sides, and there were four huge waterfalls, one in front, one behind, and one on either side. The air was filled with mist from the falling water, and the water itself pooled and swirled in a wide circular river around us.

The dragon erupted with flame, sending a sheet of red fire down on us. At the same time, two huge tunnels of water spiraled out of the rivers, swirled around Broca's staff, and shot into the air to meet the flames.

Where the fire and water met, a cloud of steam and cooling lava spiraled in perpetual explosion. It lasted for several deafening seconds, then suddenly stopped. The fire flamed out, the remaining water fell and splashed across the white stone, and the dragon sat down. It glared at Broca with an expression that was equal parts restless energy and resignation, like a caged lion.

"I don't believe it," Tav whispered.

"A dragon," I said. "You have a *dragon* in your cellar."

Tav began to laugh, then stopped himself, eyeing the

great beast before us, which was now flicking its massive tail back and forth. "A dragon? Are you serious? That is a draculadon. Lord of the dragon race. Isn't it? I mean, I can't believe I'm actually seeing one. They are supposed to be extinct."

Broca gave him an approving nod.

"I don't get it," I said. "First, why would you want to kill something so rare and beautiful? Second, if you can capture it, you can kill it, so why don't you just get on with it instead of making us do it?"

CAN I? I HAVE HAD THIS DRACULADON IMPRISONED FOR YEARS. IF I COULD KILL IT, I WOULD HAVE DONE SO. AS FOR MY REASONS, THEY ARE JUST THAT. MINE. ALL YOU NEED TO KNOW IS THAT YOU MUST DO THIS THING FOR ME. IF YOU SUCCEED, I WILL HELP YOU AND TEACH YOU. IF YOU FAIL, YOU KNOW THE CONSEQUENCES.

He handed the flaming staff to Tav, who held it gingerly, surprised that the flames didn't hurt him.

THE GROAN WILL OBEY YOUR WISHES AS MY OWN. THE STAFF WILL COME WHEN YOU NEED IT AND DO YOUR BIDDING, BUT ONLY IN HERE. THERE'S NO GOING BACK, OF COURSE, NOT FOR EITHER OF YOU. YOU KNOW MY SECRET NOW. THAT I POSSESS SUCH A BEAST AND SEEK TO KILL IT. SUCH KNOWLEDGE COMES WITH A PRICE, AND THE PRICE IS YOUR LIFE. THERE IS NO GOING BACK. FAIL ME, AND

THERE IS NO GOING FORWARD. PROVE YOUR WORTH NOW.
YOU HAVE TWO DAYS.

With that, the wizard vanished, leaving us quite alone with the Dragon.[40]

"Okay, Simon," Tav said. "Any bright ideas?" The dragon, seeing that Broca had gone, rose to its feet once more, eyeing the two of us curiously.

"I'm pretty sure our little friend there is about to test us. Do you know how to use that thing?"

"Uh," Tav said, eyeing the staff. His hands were shaking.

"Here it comes!"

The dragon bellowed and lit the air with a new gust of flame.

"WAHHHGALAGAKIN!" Tav screamed. "MAGIC STAFF, DO THAT THING YOU DID WITH BROCA AND THE WATER AND DON'T LET US DIE!"

Just as before, water flew from the river, wrapped around the staff, and shot to meet the fire, extinguishing it in midair. The stream rose and widened, pushing the fire back into the dragon's mouth and covering the beast with water. The water abated, and the dragon shook itself and sat back in frustration.

"Nice one," I said.

Tav lifted his chin proudly. "It's all about knowing the right words."

---

40 I don't care what they say. That's what it was. A dragon by any other name would still eat meat. Or something like that…

The dragon shook itself like a dog, creating a temporary rainstorm. I mention this because during the ducking and covering that we did, I happened to see something small and golden flash around the dragon's neck. Tav did as well.

"Isn't that precious?" Tav said. "It has a necklace."

"Do dragons not usually wear necklaces?"

"Draculadons. And no, they do not usually touch anything made by men, or so I've read."

"Right. So, level with me, Tav. How powerful are you? How much do you actually know about draculadons? I guess what I'm asking is: How do you like our chances of defeating this thing?"

"Uh," Tav said. "I'm okay. Pretty far beyond okay, actually, especially for my age. That's what my dad says. As for draculadons, not much is really known. I've read a book, but it wasn't about draculadons specifically. It was about Titans. You know, beasts of incredible magic that we don't really understand? How about you?"

It didn't seem like the right time to tell him that I was the most powerful wizard that would ever live. Especially because I wasn't yet.[41] "Yeah. Same. So we don't stand much chance of doing in two days what Broca has failed to do in *years*."

"Oh, we're *going* to do it," Tav said. "Trust me. I've wanted a master like Broca all my life. I'm not going to let a little thing like impossibility[42] get in my way."

---

41 Life can be frustrating during that portion of it when you have not yet become yourself. Am I right? I'm talking to you, teenagers.

42 "Never tell me the odds!" —Han Solo

"Cool," I said. "But right now, I propose a different plan."

"What's that?"

"Skedaddle."

"Yeah?" Tav glanced back at the dragon,[43] which had stealthily risen to its feet and was now towering over us, openmouthed. The necklace hung down on a long gold chain, and I saw an unmistakable flash of red from the stone it held. After squeaking in such a girlish way that my residual feelings of unmanliness were completely ameliorated,[44] Tav raised the magic staff and shouted, "LET'S GO! LET'S GO GO GO GOOOO!"

He was still wincing and shouting "OOO" when we appeared quite suddenly in the room above. I bent forward to look into the Groan and found a brilliant blue eye staring back at me. Careful not to shriek, squeak, or feminate[45] in any way, I snapped the lid closed and stepped back.

"Nice magicking," I said.

"Thanks."

"Very dignified."

Tav grinned. He raised the staff and frowned at it.

---

43 Word to the wise: If you're ever trapped in a confined space with a *dragon*, don't take your eyes off it.

44 Pardon me. I had a vocabulary sneeze. Translation: I felt better about myself.

45 Feminate (FEM-i-nate) is not a word anymore. When it *was* a word, it was an adjective that meant feminine. However, it *should* clearly be a verb that means to do something girly, so that's how I use it. You should too.

"Should we leave this thing here, or carry it around with us?"

At his words, the staff shrank in size until it lay in the palm of his hand like a ballpoint pen. He set it on top of the box.

"That'll work," I said, then indicated the ladder. "After you?"

We started to climb, and Tav spoke softly. "Something bothers me."

"You mean, other than that we're enslaved to an evil wizard and that we've been pitted against each other with our lives on the line and tasked with killing a Titan?"

"Yeah, other than that. It's that necklace."

My skin prickled.

"I mean, it's not natural, is it? Maybe that necklace is part of what makes the Groan work, but I don't think so."

"No?"

"No," he said. "I think that necklace might be what Broca wants. Apart from the starheart, obviously.

"The starheart?"

"Sure," Tav said. "I mean, not much is known about draculadons, but we certainly know why a wizard would want to kill one.

"We do?"

Tav stopped short. "Simon, are you sure you're a wizard at all?"

"Pretty sure," I said. "Draculadons are obviously my weak point."

"Perfect," Tav said. "Anyway, Broca wants to harvest

the draculadon's starheart. A draculadon heart is supposed to be made of pure magic, containing more raw magical energy than a star. Hence the name. Obviously, Broca's after that. But personally I'm more interested in that necklace. Did you see that red stone it held?"

"Why?" I said. "Why are you more interested in the necklace?"

"Well," Tav said slowly, "I figure either Broca put it there, or someone else did, and he wants it. That's probably more likely. It looked old, don't you think?"

"Why would a wizard put a necklace on a dragon?"

"*Draculadon.* Isn't it obvious? For safekeeping. Anyone can find something you've hidden. Anyone can break into a safe. But how many people can steal something from around the neck of a draculadon?"

"Not many," I admitted.

"Not many," he agreed. "But we're going to."

"I suppose we are," I said.

Of course, I had known I would have to steal the necklace from the moment I saw it. Tav was right and wrong at the same time: It *was* old, in my time. Here on Tarinea, it technically hadn't even been made yet. The bloodstone—for that's what it was, without a doubt—wouldn't be given to Rok for a long time yet, and this certainly was only a piece of it. One of the lost stones. That meant that it had been hidden here for me to find. I had found another missing bloodstone, and draculadons, evil wizards, and frenemies notwithstanding, I had to get it.

Back in the lab, Sipher was waiting for us. Broca was nowhere in sight.

THE MASTER COMMENDS YOU FOR SURVIVING YOUR FIRST ENCOUNTER WITH THE DRACULADON. HE HAS OTHER BUSINESS IN THE CITY TODAY AND SHALL BE AWAY FOR SOME TIME. YOU ARE FREE TO PURSUE WHATEVER MEANS OF DRACULADON SLAYING SEEMS MOST EXPEDIENT TO YOU. YOU SHOULD ALSO KNOW THAT THERE ARE CERTAIN FORCES IN THIS CITY THAT ARE VERY... CURIOUS ABOUT THE CONTENTS OF BROCA'S GROAN. AS SUCH, YOUR NEW KNOWLEDGE MIGHT PLACE YOU IN SOME DANGER. LASTLY, I AM TO INFORM YOU THAT YOU WERE FOLLOWED HERE BY SOME SORT OF SPY, WHO IS NOW WATCHING YOU FROM BEHIND THE BICORN EMULSION VAT. GOOD LUCK.

With that, Sipher rotated ninety degrees, flashed a light at us, and zoomed up through the open roof into the sky.

A wise man seldom wishes to see the future. His most important work is in the present, and the past and future are at best, distractions, at worst, looming monsters.

—Yeliab J. Nitsua[46]

Tav and I spun around to face the large steel tank with the picture of a two-horned unicorn-looking thing taped to the side.

"All right," I said, slipping my hand inside the turncoat. "We know you're hiding back there. Come out, or we'll roast you like a turducken!"[47]

"Hold on a minute!" an aged voice croaked from behind the vat. "Don't kill me!" One grayish horn peeked out, then a very small, very ancient minotaur stepped into view. Though obviously fully grown, he was so old that the former strength and vitality of youth had long since

46 I can't remember who he is, but if I remember right his name spells something backwards…

47 A chicken stuffed inside a duck, stuffed inside a turkey. In England, they do it with a goose, and call it *Gooducken*. How neat is that? By the way, *turducken* is a portmanteau (port-MAN-toe), which means a word that is made up of other words blended together. Other examples: smoke + fog = smog, motor + hotel = motel, velvet + crochet = velcro, veritas + horizon = Verizon. (*veritas* is Latin for truth)

wasted away, and he was now no bigger than Drake.

"Simon," the minotaur rasped, leaning forward on a small cane. "It's me."

"Me?" I said slowly.

The old minotaur pulled Drake's sling out of his pocket and brandished it. "Simon, it's *me*."

"He's got a weapon!" Tav shouted.

Most unfortunately, the unexpected appearance of Ancient Drake had completely blown my mind cone, leaving me too stunned to intervene as Tav cupped his hands together and then pulled them apart, forming a two-foot-wide purple fireball.

"Simon!" Ancient Drake shouted as Tav launched the fireball at him.

Seeing that I was too busy being surprised to come to his rescue, Drake raised the cane into the air, and it transformed into a *huge* golden sword, which he used to sever the fireball in half. The two halves swirled around him and struck the side of the vat, incinerating the picture of the bicorn.

"Whoa," I said.

"If you throw another Vioplasm at me, young man," Drake wheezed, pointing his cane at Tav (it had become a cane again almost immediately), "I will shave that blond tousled head of yours and weave myself a pair of little yellow socks."

Tav hesitated, holding another fireball aloft. "What?"

"It's okay," I said, bumping Tav's elbow. "I know him. I think. Drake, why... How..."

"Why am I so old and frail? How did I follow you

hundreds of years into the past?"

"Yeah."

"Did you feel me grab hold of you in the tomb of Rone, right when you turned E6?"

"Uh…maybe. I thought you did, but then you weren't here with me, so I figured…"

"Ah," Drake said, shuffling closer. "Well, I *did* grab hold of you, and Tessa caught hold of me. And I held on to you as you journeyed here. I held on almost the entire way."

"*Almost* the entire way?"

"Yep. I finally slipped off, right before you arrived."

"So…"

"Simon, what do you think happens when multiple people are traveling through a magical space-time portal together and some of them slip out a little early?"

"Uh…they arrive late?"

"They arrive *early,* Simon."

"Wait a minute, that doesn't make any sense." I was looking at Drake now, his ancient three-inch-long eyebrows, his tangled white beard, his drooping skin. "So…um…how long have you been here?"

Drake snorted, and his ancient cow moustache billowed outward in the breeze. "Eighty years, Simon. We've been here for eighty years."

My mouth hung open in a state of utter flabbergastation.[48]

48 Not a word.

What did he say? Eighty years? My friends had been here, in Tarinea, for *eighty* years? They had lived a whole lifetime without me? I had trapped my best friends in the past for *eighty years???* What did that mean? What did—

"Wait a minute," I said. This didn't feel right. I crossed to where Drake was leaning on his cane and kicked the stick out from under him. He stumbled slightly, but rather than collapsing like an old man, he caught himself and laughed.

"All right," he said, grinning. "I knew you wouldn't believe it, but Tessa made me promise to try. She said you had done something so stupid that you deserved to feel horrified for a little while." Drake rubbed his face as if washing it with soap, and his appearance changed. Soon, he was his normal puny adolescent self again.

"What in the name of Times New Roman is going on?" Tav demanded. "Who are you? Simon, do you know this minotaur?"

"Ha!" I laughed, embracing my friend. "Yeah, I know him, Tav. This is my best friend. I forgot to mention, but I sort of traveled here from the distant future. I thought I was alone, but apparently my friends came with me!"

Tav looked suspicious. "I knew there was something strange about you, but I didn't think it was that."

"Do you believe me?" I asked.

Tav shrugged. "I guess so. But, sorry, but are minotaurs, uh… I mean, in the future, are they… Well, you said he's your friend, right?"

Drake chuckled. "Simon, you should know that in

the time of Tarinea's existence, minotaurs were roaming the galaxy, destroying civilizations, eating people, and otherwise devouring the universe with despotic barbarism. Back then—back *now*, I mean, minotaurs were killed on sight by pretty much everyone. That is why my disguise is so nonthreatening. Old and frail, you know. I am currently posing as a conscientious dissenter from my race, claiming that I was cast out for refusing to participate in their massacres. Some people still want to kill me here, of course, but many of the Tarineans can be reasonable."

"Right," I said, sitting down on a stool and rubbing my forehead. "So how long have you *really* been here?"

"About three months."

"Three months?"

"Better than eighty years, don't you think? You'd be amazed how much you—well, *I*—can learn with three months to explore the capitol of the magical renaissance in its prime. You won't believe what I've discovered, Simon. I could write a book. I could write ten books!"

"How did you find me?" I said.

Drake grinned. "It was Tessa's idea. She said that when you arrived—we were pretty sure you would arrive eventually—you would probably get yourself into a bunch of trouble right away, so all we had to do was figure out what the worst thing was that could happen to you, and that's where you would be." He grinned. "Guess she was right!" He elbowed me in the ribs. "By the way, nice job defeating that humdrungelob. Couldn't help noticing that you used the de-tonguing hug method described by Loquacious Bright. Last time you complain about my homework assignments, eh?"

"I was kind of hoping you hadn't seen that," I admitted. "But Drake, where's Tessa?" I glanced around, wondering if she might be hiding around a corner somewhere.

Drake's face fell. "Ah…yes. No, she's not here, Simon. I mean, she's here. She just couldn't come with me."

"Why not?"

"Well." Drake tugged at his collar uncomfortably. "You have to understand, Tessa and I fell out of a tempapstemial wormhole, which is a dangerous thing to do. I came though unscathed—which is amazing by the way. Tessa…"

"Drake," I said, feeling a growing sense of foreboding. "Tell me what's wrong with Tessa."

He sighed, shoulders slumping. "You better just see for yourself."

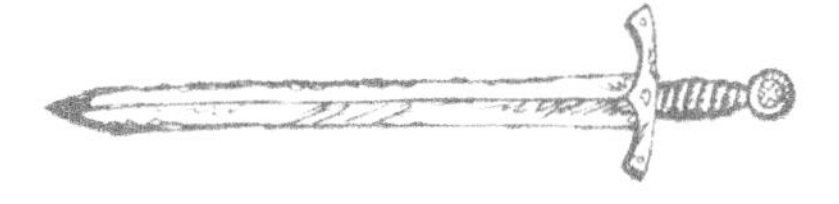

Tav and I followed Drake out of the factory and down the hill. He shuffled slowly (since he had to don his disguise again before going out in public) through the meandering streets and alleyways of the industrial section and out into the calmer, pleasant rows of white stone houses in the residential quarter.

As we walked, Drake talked. He attempted to summarize every exciting thing that he had learned about Tarinea, most of which I didn't understand. A lot of it apparently had to do with the city itself, which was obviously a bit of a mystery to modern wizard historians due to the fact that Tarinea was wiped off the face of the planet by an asteroid (allegedly).

"But," Drake was saying, "I'm not even sure if *that's* true, either! I mean, there's enough intrigue, politics, and internal power struggle going on in this place that it wouldn't surprise me if Tarinea actually ended up being destroyed by magical warfare. That rarely happens, you know, magical warfare on a large scale, because it is so devastating. But if it did, it could easily replicate the effects of a celestial collision! In fact, it's plausible that in such an event there might be no survivors to tell the real tale of what happened."

"Wow, Drake. That's super cool," I said.

"But I haven't told you the best part yet! Simon, you realize, we are living *pre-breaking*! Rok hasn't met the Zohar yet, which means Rone and Rellik haven't started fighting, and Rone hasn't broken magic yet, and everyone who lives here still has access to all six branches of magic! It's incredible! You wouldn't believe what these wizards can do!"

"Tav?" I said.

The boy had stopped walking and was standing quite alone now, several feet behind us, staring at the ground.

"Huh?" He glanced up, as if waking from a dream.

"You okay?"

He looked at me blankly. "You just said that these people, Rok, Rellik, and… Who was the other one?"

"Rone," Drake said.

"Right. Did you just tell me that these people are going to alter magic *itself*, and that Tarinea is going to be destroyed in some kind of war?"

"Oh," Drake said. "Ohhh. Right." He looked suddenly nervous. "I'm sorry. Terribly insensitive of us to tell you all that. You, uh, really can't tell anyone what you just heard, okay?"

Tav's blank expression was fading into a grin now. "Who would believe me anyway, right? So, are you guys here to stop these people, then?"

"What?" I said. I turned to Drake. "I don't think so. Are we?"

"NO!" Drake was holding up his hands in protest, looking quite horrified, as if I had suggested that we let someone borrow one of his books. "No, no, no, no! We absolutely must *not* try to alter the past! In some ways, what we're doing here is uncharted territory, but this much is clear from the literature: Purposely altering the past almost *always* results in complete chaos."

"Calm down, cowboy," I said, employing Tessa's favorite nickname.

Tav forced us to stop and tell him what was going on. I thought Drake would have a long, complicated argument complete with the top ten reasons you can't tell people living in the past about what's coming in the future, but instead he answered Tav's questions pretty succinctly.

We were from the future. At some point in Tarinea's near future, a wizard named Rok would use the special power of a magical bloodstone gifted to him by a race of godlike light-dwellers called the Zohar to reweave the flows of magic so that only morally principled wizards could have magical power. After that, his good-for-nothing grandson would force him to reweave magic again, making wizards much less powerful, in the hope that he could rule over them.

But Rok was able to partially thwart his grandson's plan, letting the other brother, Rellik, have extra power, and cutting off Rone's power instead. Rok broke the magical bloodstone into fifty pieces, scattered them across the galaxy, and the two grandsons spent hundreds of years trying to locate them, one hoping to regain his power, the other hoping to protect the universe from the evil his brother was trying to unleash. Rellik had died a while back, and now I (Simon), his pseudo-heir, was continuing his work.[49]

When we had finished explaining, Tav looked like he was going to be sick.

"Maybe we shouldn't have told him any of this," Drake said.

"No," Tav said, forcing his face back into a normal expression. "It's okay. I'd rather know than not know. You know?"

"No," Drake said. "Not really, but we'll take your word for it. You still want to come along?"

Tav shrugged, and we continued on the way we had

49 If you're wondering. Yes. That was a sneaky way to reiterate the plot to you, the reader, as well.

been going. He spoke even less now, and he seemed to be lost in dark thoughts of his own. I tried to imagine what it would be like knowing that my civilization was doomed, and that the world as I had always known it was destined to change for the worse.

Poor Tav. There was nothing he could do about it, really, other than sit around and wait. We didn't know when this calamity would befall Tarinea, of course, but I began hoping that Tav had enough time to grow up and get away from it all. I glanced around at what people I could see, realizing that they all might be doomed to die in the near future. I frowned.

"Drake, where are all these people going?"

The people on the street were walking from house to house. They would disappear inside one, then others would come out of it and walk to the next house, or the one after that, and then disappear inside. "Is there some sort of neighborhood block party going on, err…everywhere?"

Drake chuckled. "Tarinea is a *big* city, Simon. So big that environmental conservation, as well as security, are real concerns. There are sixty-eight different sectors of the city, really. Each one is accessed through magical entrances within these houses. That way, each one has one entrance and exit that can be guarded, and the city never grows physically larger than what you see out here. Of course, all you see here is the *old* Tarinea. The old industrial sector, the graveyard, the Maw. But nobody lives here except for a couple outcasts."

"Like Broca," I said.

"Like Broca," he agreed.

"So I haven't really even seen Tarinea yet," I said.

"Not even close," Tav said.

We stopped in front of one of the little white stone houses. There was a brass number "42" on the door.

"This is us," Drake said.

I opened the door and stepped into what seemed like a whole other world.

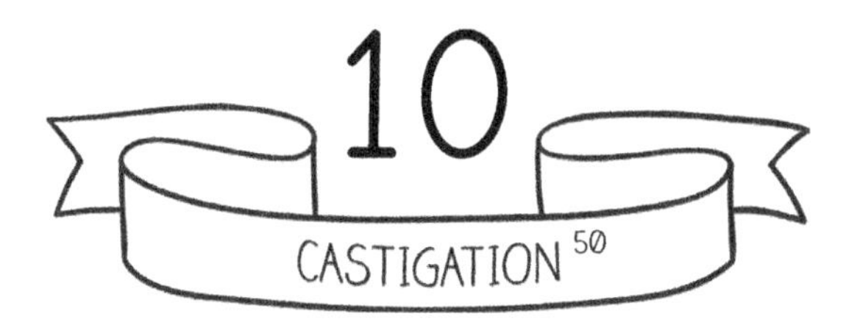

10 CASTIGATION[50]

For whom the Lord loveth, he chasteneth.

—Hebrews 12:6

Tarinea, Sector 42, was a metropolitan jungle of skyscrapers, alleyways, and towers, all interconnected by a series of strange-looking rail cars and elevator platforms. The size of it was staggering—at least as big as Manhattan—and even if it wasn't as densely populated, this city certainly held over half a million people. How many sectors had Drake said there were again? Tarinea was a big, *big* plac—

"Watch out!" Tav said and pulled me back from the edge of the little platform upon which we stood suspended over a drop of a hundred feet or so. One of the strange little rail carriages zipped by through the space in front of the platform, and the whoosh of air tousled my hair. The giant buildings, tinted red in the midmorning sun, rose around us like great trees, and we seemed to be suspended about halfway up. Glowing steel bars wound everywhere through space, like airborne spaghetti, and the little rail

50 Chastisement, punishment, correction.

carriages dangled from them, zipping along to and fro.

"We'll take this one," Drake said as a carriage came to a stop beside our platform. It was about the size of a minivan and reminded me vaguely of an underground airport train, sparse and clean. There was one other person in the carriage: a tired-looking wizard reading a newspaper. He didn't look at us or otherwise acknowledge our existence.

"I've never been to Sector 42," Tav said idly as the carriage sped away.

"Really?" I said. "I thought you grew up here."

"Nah. We've been here for a while, but I grew up…all over. Sector 42 is mostly medical services, isn't it?"

Drake nodded. The carriage sped through a tunnel that dissected one of the city's larger skyscrapers.

"Medical services?" I said. "Drake, can't you just tell me what's wrong with Tessa? Something's wrong, right? Otherwise you wouldn't be so cryptic. *She's* not like accidentally five hundred years old or anything, is she?" I shivered, imagining a wrinkly old Tessa stewing over my stupid mistakes for centuries.

Drake cleared his throat uncomfortably. "This is our stop."

He pulled a tasseled red cord that hung in the center of the carriage, and it drew up alongside a platform like the one we had just left. Back outside the carriage, I noticed that this part of the city was different than the rest. The towers were smaller, more utilitarian.

"Housing?" I guessed.

Drake nodded again. "Most of the medical staff that works in this sector choose to live close by. Tessa is staying with an old healer. A famous old healer, actually. She works for the king. We've been staying with her and her, uh...family." Drake's fur-covered cheeks went bright pink at this.

I snorted. "Sounds like this old healer has a smokin' hot minotaurian granddaughter, eh, Drake?"

Drake sneezed. "No! No. I mean, she's not a *minotaur.* Her name is Loni, and she's very nice, that's all."

"Uh-huh," Tav said.

We walked for a while down a narrow but pleasant footpath of white pavers. On either side of us, skyscrapers rose out of sight, but there were little gardens here and there and bushes nestled against the buildings, softening the atmosphere. We came to another platform, and it lifted us skyward at a leisurely pace, for which I was grateful, since there were no railings.

At the appropriate level, Drake stomped twice, and the elevator slowed to a stop, depositing us on a little entry ledge set into the side of the building. There was a surprisingly welcoming carved wooden door and a doormat woven from what looked like long green leaves. Drake placed his hand on the door, and it opened inward.

The apartment was warm and inviting, with wood floors, clean white walls, and a fresh, flowery scent on the air. There was more evidence of island life in here: a bowl of hairy brown fruit, a set of miniature trees, an intricately braided wall hanging, not unlike the doormat.

We moved down the hall and into what was unmistakably the kitchen, though it was different from any kitchen I had seen before. It was perfectly round, and the floor was covered in beach sand. In the center of the room, a chicken was roasting in a circular fire pit, and on the opposite side, a woman in her late sixties was cutting up a colorful assortment of fruit with a knife large enough to chop a cow in half.

The woman herself was small and delicate—the counters, I realized, were lower than usual to accommodate her height—and almost as colorful as the fruit she was preparing. Her skin was a rich, opalescent[51] brown, and her hair was white as the driven snow.[52]

"Grandma Loki," Drake said politely, "this is Simon, the one I was telling you about. And this is his, err... friend, Tav."

Grandma Loki spun around and walked over to us, a half-carved orange fruit in one hand and the giant cleaver in the other. She had a kindly face and rich green eyes. "Ah, yes," she said. "I am Lolialokianalli, but you can call me Grandma Loki. Everyone does. Simon and Tav... According to rumor, those are the names of Broca's new

51 Opals are a semiprecious stone known for their characteristic glowing quality. They look like they have some magical juice floating around deep down inside. I met an Egyptian girl on Earth one time with skin that was brown but somehow glowing golden underneath. This woman was a lot like that.

52 *Driven* snow falls out of the sky and is carried by the wind into drifts. It never touches the ground, rooftops, moose butts, or anything else that might make it dirty, and is therefore whiter than regular snow.

apprentices—foul, backward, armpit of a man, if you ask me, not that I'd say an unkind word about anybody. The king certainly doesn't like him. Mentioned so just yesterday. You wouldn't be *that* Simon and Tav, I suppose?"

"Uhh…" I said, eyeing the knife.

Drake sighed. "I'm afraid they are, Grandma Loki, though I don't think it was their decision, strictly speaking."

"Of course not," she said easily. "And tell me, has Broca asked you to kill anyone yet? Steal something, perhaps?"

"Well…" I hedged.

"I thought so," she said. "That's what an evil master always does first, you know. Get you to betray your conscience and trust them instead. Step one to making evil slaves."

Tav cleared his throat. "Excuse me, but just what would you know about evil masters? Or slaves, for that matter."

"I know everything, dear." She adjusted the slippery fruit in one hand and began inspecting my face with the cleaver, pushing my head this way and that, lifting my hair, tapping the coin embedded in my forehead, etc. She tilted my head back and looked in my nostrils, then tilted it forward again. Thankfully, she was using the dull parts of her knife.

"This one's every bit as interesting as you made him out to be, Drakus. But he needs a bath."

With that, she spun around, waving her cleaver toward the back of the apartment. "Your girl's where you left her, and that granddaughter of mine's around here somewhere."

"This way," Drake said, leading us promptly back into the hallway. "Oh, hi, Loni." Drake pressed his back against the wall, and a thin girl squeezed around him, carrying a pitcher of water.

"Oh," she said, looking up at me. "Hello."

I felt my jaw drop open slightly. She was quite simply seventeen times prettier than any girl I had ever seen.[53] She had her grandmother's dark skin and white hair, and eyes of cobalt blue flecked with gold.

"Uhhh guhhhh," I said.

"I'm Lolialoniakalli," she said.

"Lo la la la la la la—"

"You can call me Loni," she said. "And you are?"

In that moment, I am ashamed to say that I forgot my

---

53 Totally false, of course. In reality, there isn't that much difference between "regular" girls (of course, there is no such thing), "pretty" girls, and "*really* pretty" girls. Obviously you can't actually quantify such a thing, although unfortunately most teenage boys *think* they can, and I'm ashamed to say that I was certainly one of these. The truth is that the more you get to know a girl, the prettier she becomes (it's part of their girl magic), so that pretty soon a girl you thought wasn't that pretty to begin with actually looks prettier than all the others. Likewise, a super pretty girl can lie to you, break your heart, set fire to your bicycle, and fill your backpack with rotten avocados, and pretty soon she won't look that pretty anymore (not that that has ever happened to me). What I'm trying to say is, beauty is in the eye of the beholder, and boys are notoriously unpredictable beholders, frequently prone to delusions of grandeur, hallucinations, selective blindness and uberdramaticality. It's a fact. Sometimes it works in a girl's favor, sometimes not… By the way, I used the word "pretty" eight times in this footnote. You're welcome.

name. Panicking, I said the most impressive thing I could think of.

"Pneumonoultramicroscopicsilicovolcanokoniosis."[54]

"*That's* your name?"

"Haha," I laughed stupidly. "No. I'm Fimon Sayter. No. Slimen Faker. No, *no*—"

"SIMON FAYTER!" Tessa's voice came booming out of a room at the end of the hall. "STOP DROOLING AND GET YOUR COWARDLY, CONTEMPTABLE, CAT-BRAINED, CROSSWIRED CLOVEN KEISTER IN HERE!"[55]

"I gotta go," I said and managed to smile at her without drooling much at all.

She smiled back, gave me a pitying look, and then thankfully left before my cheeks started to burn.

"My keister is *not* crosswired," I objected as I rounded the corner into the room at the end of the hall. "It functions perfec—"

Tessa, whom I expected to find sick in bed or something, was levitating in the center of the room. At least, her top half was. Her waist was glued to a sheet of glass, apparently held in place by some sort of glowing blue goo-glue. Although she was half the size as she used to be, she was easily twice as angry as I'd ever seen her.

"Hi, Simon."

"T-T-Tessa," I stuttered. "Where's the rest of you?"

---

54 Technically the longest word in the English language. Or probably any language, for that matter. It's a type of lung disease.

55 You have to admire her alliteration.

"Oh, that," she said. "Kind of you to notice.[56] Since you ask, I expect that it is either stuck in Rone's tomb or floating in a void of space-time somewhere in the future."

"Right," I said. I spread my hands out, trying to pick up the pieces of my mess, which had clearly spiraled out of control. "Tessa, I'm very sorry about this."

"You're about to be, mister."

"Tessa, are you okay? I mean, other than… I mean… You seem to be okay, though. Right?"

"I'm just peachy, Simon. The good news is, my body isn't suffering from the amputation of my legs because technically, my legs just don't exist yet."

"Oh," I said, staring at her waist stump. "Uh, good."

"On the downside, since the BOTTOM HALF of my body is MISSING, my INSIDES keep trying to join my OUTSIDES!"

"Uh…that sounds—"

"GHASTLY, Simon! It's ghastly. It's also appalling, embarrassing, grisly, shameful, and relentlessly irritating. And it's all YOUR fault!" Tessa, whose magically levitating slab could move about, had backed me up against the wall and was leveling her finger at me.

"What were you thinking trying to run out on us like that? Don't you know that running away from your problems doesn't solve anything? Don't you know that it just MAKES THINGS WORSE?" She pointed several

56 Word to the wise: If a girl every gets so angry that she begins to alternate between polite kindness and unbridled rage, you will probably begin to wonder if you are crossing a line. Look behind you, my friend! It's too late.

times at her amputated midriff to illustrate her point.

"I didn't have a choice!" I said.

"You ALWAYS have a choice."

"I just wanted to save you. All of you!"

"How's that working out so far, champ?"

"Well, not great, but—"

"You CAN'T save us all, Simon. We *know* that. That's life! We're along for the ride because we're prepared to die to see your mission accomplished! Don't let your cowardice rob us of our bravery, or our dignity."

I stared at her, speechless. Clearly, she had been working on this reprimand for a while. My eyes began to burn in the corners, which never meant anything good. It was as if she were voicing the thoughts of my own conscience, which I realized had been trying to convict me for some time. My ears began to itch again. Perfect. As if I needed another reminder of my failures.

I left. I didn't say anything to her or anyone else. I just walked quietly down the hall and out the door. No doubt I would be back later. Much later, when I could face her. I could do it later, just not now. Of course, this was the mentality that got me into this predicament in the first place, but there you go.

I slammed the door on my way out.

That would show her.

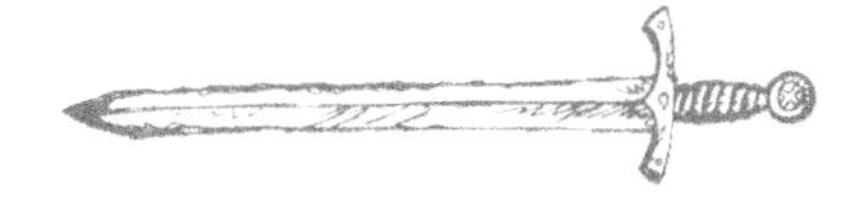

I am told that Drake, who had been hiding from Tessa's

wrathstorm in the room across the hall, went in to see her after I left and said, "Feel better?"

She didn't respond for a while, but eventually she sighed a deep, sad sigh and said, "I *may* have been too hard on him."

She made him swear never to tell anyone that.

Three things in human life are important: the first is to be kind; the second is to be kind; and the third is to be kind.

—Henry James[57]

I walked through the heart of Tarinea, Sector 42 alone. There wasn't much to see.

There was a little creek running along the valley floor, winding around the base of the housing buildings, and there was a little-used path with quaint wooden bridges that had the look of being built many years prior. The most interesting thing that happened as I walked was that my ears began to itch in a very serious fashion. I scratched them at first, but that only made it worse. Then I had the bright idea to dunk my head in the stream, thinking maybe a little water would calm them down.

Not so.

In fact, I happened to dunk my head right into the corner of a partially submerged colony of water beetles. As you can imagine, the beetles didn't thank me for that.

57 A famous British writer. Everyone says his books are very influential, but I've never met someone who has read one.

Naturally, these were *biting* beetles, so my walk turned into a run for a while.

At length, I found a little restaurant set into the base of one of the high rises. It didn't look very popular, but it had a nice deck that stretched out over the stream. It was barely noon, and the place seemed to have just opened.

I plopped down at a table on the deck, and a plump lady bustled out to take my order. Realizing that I had no money, I asked if I could just sit a while.

"Sure, dearie," she said. A minute later, she brought me a steaming hot mug of brown stuff.

"But I can't pay..."

"There are bigger problems than that in the world, dearie." She winked at me and disappeared again.

Well, wasn't that the truth. Still, it felt nice. The unexpected kindness of strangers usually does.

My ears were itching even worse now, and it was taking all of my self-control not to jump on top of the table and begin screaming and ripping my hair out.

I took a sip of the brown stuff and spat it out. It was both hot and foul. I had a brief mental image of Drake laboring over a hot stove for several hours to make it, adding in dead rats and pesto and rotten apple cider. He'd probably like it.

I frowned at the thought of him, and my ears itched, if possible, even more. Usually the itching relented after a while, but apparently the Zohar were trying to teach me a lesson. Either that or they were just bored today.

The table was a bit dusty, and I started to draw in it.

Soon I found myself writing out my code.

I will be my best self.

Well, that wasn't going very well, was it? I had abandoned my friends in their moment of need and was trying to hide from my problems. In my heart of hearts, I knew what I had to do. I knew, and I was running anyway. I hadn't even been able to face Tessa when she confronted me with the truth.

I will honor my word.

How many promises had I broken lately? Not sure. Maybe that wasn't as bad as the others, but still, not good.

I will help those I can.

Don't even get me started on that one.

I will never give up.

Yikes. Can you say *catastrophe*?

As if to illustrate the point just then, my right ear, which had begun to burn as well as itch, dropped off.

I mean that literally. It just...*dropped* off the side of my head. It hit the deck with a sad little *flarp* noise, and I stared down at it, thinking of the story Tessa had told long ago (only a few days ago, actually, but it *seemed* like a lifetime) of her uncle Darion, whose arms disappeared one day after he repeatedly ignored his code.

I reached for my ear, but just as I was about to pick it up, a bird swooped down and snatched it up, carrying it off into the sky.

I sighed, reaching up to scratch my other ear. It came off in my hand, and I set it on the table. I eyed my ear dubiously. I deserved this, I suppose. The poetic justice was not lost on me. I was ignoring my conscience. I refused to *hear* its prodding, and so, if I wasn't going to use my ears, the Zohar were going to take them. Fitting.

"You look busy," a voice said.

Loni was there, beside the table, looking at my ear. Her hair practically glowed in the sunlight, it was so white.

I got to my feet and pulled a chair out for her. "Not at all. Thoughtful, perhaps. *Ear*itated, maybe, but not busy. How on earth did you find me?"

She gave me a guilty smirk. "I may have followed you. Sorry. I, uh…overheard what Tessa said. Figured you could use a friend right about now. Also, Drake told me to follow you and tell you to come back." She slid into a chair across from me and eyed my ear critically. "Do you have some sort of disease? I've never heard of anything like that. I'm training with my grandmother, you know. Apprenticed at the castle, in fact. But I've never seen anything like *that*."

I stared at her blankly, then realized that she had no idea what the Zohar were and knew nothing about wizard codes, as that was all far in the future still. "Oh no," I said. "I just broke a promise, you know, and this is my punishment."

"Harsh," she said, nodding. "But then, it's not good to break your promises."

"No," I agreed.

There was an awkward silence, and then she looked into my cup. "Oh! You like punjilak? It's one of my favorites."

"Actually, I think I've lost my taste for it."

"Shame," she said, eyeing the cup hungrily.

I grinned. "Help yourself."

"Thanks." She gulped down half of the disgusting brown liquid and nestled back into her chair, shivering in pleasure.

I laughed. "You and Drake would get along well," I said.

She blushed. "You think so? I like him. He's very... polite."

"Oh," I said, taken aback.[58] "Yeah, he's the best. He likes disgusting— I mean, he likes a *variety* of foods, so he would probably like eating here, if you wanted to bring him."

She twirled a finger in her hair. "I just might have to do that. You know, he's been living in my home for weeks now, and he barely looks at me. I know why, of course. But he won't stop talking, and he only talks about one thing. You know what it is?"

"Minotaurian Yakrat Androgotincture?" I guessed.

"No. *You*. All he ever talks about is you. Simon this. Simon that. I think I've heard all your adventures at least three times."

"Ugh. Sorry."

"That's okay. Is it true you're from the future? And you're here because you're trying to find a way to save your friends?"

58 It's not like I was surprised that she liked him more than me, okay. I'm not *that* kind of friend. I was just surprised about, you know... something else.

"Pretty much."

"Then maybe you shouldn't feel so bad about yourself. Sounds like you're doing the right thing to me."

I glanced down at my ear just as a beetle landed on it. It was ruby red and about the size of my thumbnail. It was also apparently very hungry, because it began munching on my earlobe.

"A crick beetle!" Loni exclaimed. "That's lucky!"

"I don't know what luck has to do with it. I put my whole head into a pile of the things a few minutes ago."

"Really?" She put her hands over her mouth. "That's *very* lucky."

"Good," I said. "I'm going to need it."

"Grandma Loki doesn't like your new friend much," Loni said. "Tav, I think his name is."

"Yeah." I rubbed my head. "I'm not sure what I think about him either, but for now, I'm stuck with him."

"Hmm. Made some more promises or something?" She was looking at my ear again.

"No, he's my fellow slave, and one of us needs to kill the other one, or else find a loophole. That's *after* we defeat a draculadon together."

She gave a low whistle. "How do you intend to do that?"

"No idea," I said.

"Do you really have to kill it?"

I shrugged. "I'd rather not, but it's sort of it or me, right now, and it has something else I need."

"Sounds complicated."

"You have no idea," I said, grinning.

"Probably not," she agreed. She cleared her throat. "You know, you can't stay away forever. The others have probably already concocted a plan."

"Yeah?"

"Sure. It's been like an hour, and they've been researching for weeks just to be ready to help you out."

"All right," I said. "Is Tessa still angry?"

"Oh, I think she will be angry for quite a while, Simon. But that's no reason to stay away."

"Right," I said, rising to my feet.

She polished off the remainder of her punjilak and followed me back down the path.

"So why did Drake send *you* to bring me back?" I asked.

"Isn't it obvious?" she said, batting her eyes at me. "I'm gorgeous. He figured you couldn't say no."

"Right," I said. "But you like *Drake*, right?"

She laughed. "I don't know. Does it matter?"

I shrugged. It felt odd, worrying about little things like Drake and girls, with my friends' lives—not to mention the fate of the universe—hanging in the balance. But it felt good too. As usual, the small everyday things were what gave the big stuff meaning.

"I'll warn you," Loni said. "I don't know exactly what kind of plan your friends are hatching, but the bits and pieces I've overheard… The people they talk about… Well. It sounds dangerous. I'm not so sure I'd go running toward danger like that if I were you."

"That's pretty much my only hobby," I said, giving her my best hero wink. "The truth is, whether I run toward it or away from it, danger usually finds me either way."

Plans are often hatched the same way eggs are: by a bunch of chickens sitting around, talking.

—Yeliab J. Nitsua

Simon, have you misplaced your ears?"

Back at Grandma Loki's, lunch was served. Tessa, of course, had noticed my little issue. Okay, okay. My ears were gone. *Everyone* had noticed my little issue.

"Technically one of them is in my pocket," I said.

"What happened, man?" Drake said.

Tessa cleared her throat. If she was trying not to grin, she was failing big time. "Having a little Zohar problem?" she guessed.

I didn't answer, and they stopped asking. We sat on the sand around the firepit eating fresh fruit and roast chicken and rice, and somehow eating on the ground wasn't strange at all. I spent most of the time doing my best not to look at Loni or Tessa, which wasn't easy.

Drake and Tav helped out by spending most of the meal arguing. Apparently Drake had been neck deep in research about how pre-breaking magic functioned and had come up with a theory about how channeling vessels worked as well. Tav was now telling him that he was completely wrong.

"It's not that magic can't be controlled without a channeling vessel," Tav said.

"Then surely it is untouchable," Drake said. "You can't touch your magic without a vessel. Just like Simon here can't touch his without the turncoat."

"Hey, leave me out of it," I said.

"No," Tav said. "The only thing a channeling vessel does is help you focus."

Drake folded his arms. "You're lying."

"Why would he lie, Drake?" Tessa said around a mouthful of chicken.

"He speaks the truth," Grandma Loki said. "I am not much for the use of magic, but even I know this."

"Fine," Drake said. "It helps you focus what, then? Focus yourself or focus the magic?"

"What's the difference?" Tav said.

"Bookman Old Style!" Drake swore. "What do you mean, what's the difference?"

"Sorry," Tav said. "My grandfather used to lecture me about this. It just slipped out. He says magic stems from the soul itself, and it isn't useful to think about them as being separate. He says a channeling vessel is a shortcut unbefitting real wizards. That's why I don't have one."

"You don't?" Drake said, looking disappointed.

"Nope."

"Who cares, anyway," Tessa said, setting her empty bowl down on the ground. "We have plans to hatch. I'm done, so you all might as well be too. Thanks for the food, Grandma Loki. Wonderful as always. Please excuse us now, as we need a bit of time to talk. With any luck, we'll be out of your hair in no time."

"No trouble at all, dear," Grandma Loki said. "Stay as long as you like."

Tessa's levitating slab rose to waist height and floated down the hallway toward the room I had first found her in. I stared down at my half-eaten food and set it down in dismay. I had kind of wanted to finish. Truth be told, I had wanted to hear the rest of that conversation about channeling vessels too. I was pretty certain that the turncoat was acting as my channeling vessel, so it made sense to learn as much as I could about it.

"She won't like it if we make her wait," Drake pointed out, setting down his own bowl. "She's been in a bad mood ever since… You know…" He gestured at his waist, and I nodded.

Tav, Drake, and I joined Tessa in the back room a minute later. Loni said she wanted to help her grandmother clean up, and Drake whispered to me later that she might as well not know what we were up to. "The less she knows, the safer she is." He blushed when he said this, and I wondered if he knew that she liked him, or if that was just his normal amount of blushing.

"While you've been dawdling," Tessa said when I entered the room, "we've been busy." She pointed at one wall of the room, which was covered by large sheets of paper filled with charts and notes in Drake's handwriting.

"Drake's work has been largely dedicated to a study of channeling vessels in the hopes that he could help you figure out how to best utilize the turncoat."

I perked up at this, but Drake was scowling again.

"Of course," Tessa continued, "he has been largely hampered in this work by the delicate nature of the research. You can't just walk up to someone and ask ridiculously simple questions about magic without drawing suspicion. Today, it seems, Tav here has overthrown some of Drake's principle assumptions, so much of his theory may now be..." She hesitated.

"Useless," Drake finished, staring daggers at Tav.

Tav shrugged. "Sorry."

"*Anyway,*" Tessa cut in, "Drake has also been inserting himself into the public life of Tarinea. He is fairly well known now, and many people like the rambling old minotaur persona, despite the loathsome nature of his race."

"Hey!" Drake protested.

"Nice," I said, ignoring him. "That might prove useful."

"Meanwhile," Tessa continued, "my studies have been focused on the purpose of your visit here, which I presume to be in two parts." She held up her fingers to count. "First, you came here looking for a solution to the dilemma on Cathagorous, so I have been compiling a list of the wisest and most powerful residents of Tarinea, in case you wanted to consult with them." She pointed to a wall that held numerous cut-out pictures and profiles of people.

"Excellent!" I said. "Tessa, that's perfect!"

"Yes, I know," she said. "Top of the list is King Diamar. He is widely known to be a wise and brilliant man. In fact, he apparently locks himself away studying obscure things, writing books, writing laws, and consulting wizards in need of advice. He pretty much lets his daughter Hiamene run the kingdom while he does all that."

As she spoke, she pointed from a painting of a regal-looking wizard to a sketch of the young woman who had sentenced us to be Broca's slaves. "Second on the list is Broca, an outcast by all accounts, but clearly brilliant, which is probably why people hate him. He might be a bit evil too, but it's hard to tell. He's definitely dangerous. I'm not surprised you ended up as his slave. Nice forehead coin, by the way. Do you think you can get him to give you advice?"

"Maybe," I said. "But I have to kill some things first."

"Including me, probably," Tav said.

"Right," I agreed.

"I see," Tessa said, frowning. "Well, my third option is Xerith. He's supposed to be unaccountably wise. A seer—or whatever they called seers before the breaking—by the sounds of it. But he's also supposed to be crazy. And he's impossible to find. In fact, he's more of a legendary being, and he might not even live on Tarinea at all." She sighed, indicating a picture that wasn't a picture at all, more an outline of a head with a big question mark where the face should be.

"Sounds about right," I said.

"The second thing I've been studying is this," she

said, moving to a different wall. "I presume that since the turncoat brought you here, there might be a bloodstone here for you to locate. You did come here by turning E6, right?"

I nodded.

"And you still have a bloodstone in the pocket of E6, don't you?"

I nodded again.

"Well, if we find a bloodstone here, then it will serve as further proof of a theory that I've been working on."

"Oh," Drake cut in, "you'll like this Simon. It's super cool."

"Quiet, Drake," Tessa said, but she was smiling. "The theory is that the turncoat actually takes you to a location connected with whatever you place in the pocket. Or, perhaps, to another item like the one you place in the pocket. You had a bloodstone in it, so the first time you turned it, it took you to Daru. Into the very room where another bloodstone was hidden, actually.

"The second time you turned it, it took you back, but technically it was also taking you to a place where several bloodstones were located: Skelligard. If I'm right, then since it brought you here, there is a bloodstone hidden here as well, though I didn't realize that Rok might have hidden them in other time periods."

I grinned. "Tessa, you're brilliant." I had been thinking the same thing, sort of. I felt like I was here to find another bloodstone, but I didn't know why or how the process worked, and she had figured it out.

Tessa blushed. "Well, we don't know if I'm right yet. Still, I have been compiling a list of the most likely locations to find it." She pointed at the third wall, which was covered with several large maps that had been circled in dozens of places and covered in notes.

"Tessa," I said.

"Don't interrupt," Tessa said. "I've been working hard at this. Some of the most likely places include the royal treasury, the official depository of Tarinea, and the museum of ancient magics. Those possibilities, of course, presume that someone found the bloodstone and sensed that it was something important. If, however, Rok *hid* it here hoping no one would find it, it could be anywhere. Which leads me to the list of top hiding places."

"Tessa," I said again.

"Hush. First is the dead quarter. As you might have noticed, a quarter of the city is a cemetery. It's a complex, convoluted labyrinth of tombs and underground catacombs. The perfect place to hide something for hundreds of years without anyone finding it."

"But, Tessa…" I said.

"I know, I know," Tessa said, straightening her hair in annoyance. "That would take forever to search. Which is why I have also listed 'architecture' in my top places to hide things. It occurs to me that sometimes the best hiding places are in plain sight, so Rok might have incorporated the stone into some sort of statue or structure, right where people look at it so much they stop seeing it. That's what I would have done. A third possibility is—"

"Tessa, I've already found it."

She froze, staring at me in amazement. "Already?"

"Yeah."

"But, you've been here for like five minutes!"

"Yeah... I think it's *my* turn to tell a story," I said, and I began to relate all that I had done since appearing in Tarinea. Tessa and Drake were a perfect audience. Tav did a lot of yawning. Tessa broke into my story at the appropriate points and pulled out her diagram of the turncoat pockets, complete with labels.

To be accurate, she took out an exact *copy* of her diagram, since the original sketch was in her pants pocket, and her pants were still, presumably, housing her legs somewhere in the future.

Nevertheless, she now labeled D2 *Cover.* It had made the fart noise, and we guessed that since it made a sheep fall from the sky earlier, it was the mystery knob that had done the same thing back on Daru. So while we weren't a hundred percent sure what it would do next, it seemed like it would be useful in situations where I needed to cause a distraction. She tentatively labeled A7 *Epiphany* because it had caused me to have a stroke of brilliance during my confrontation with Broca.

"No," I said. "Let's call that one *Stroke.*"

"Why would we do that?" Tessa said icily.

"Because it's cooler?" I said. "And that's what it does. It gives me a stroke of brilliance."

Tessa scowled. "But stroke can mean so many different things. It's a... What do you call them? A homonym. You can stroke a cat. You can die from a stroke. You can have a stroke of brilliance. *Epiphany,* on the other hand, has only one meaning. So that's what we're going to name it."

"Geez," I said. "Are you going to be this picky about everything?"

"Does it matter?"

"Nope." I cleared my throat. "Speaking of things that don't matter, I feel I should point out that we might not actually know what this knob does. I mean, with me being brilliant all the time, it's kind of hard to tell when something is making me *more* brilliant."

She smacked me.

Things were getting back to normal.

When we had finished, Tav poked me in the chest. "You didn't let on that you knew that necklace was your bloodstone."

"Didn't want to overwhelm you with a long story just then," I said. The truth was, of course, that at the time I was disturbed by his cleverness[59] and hadn't yet decided to trust him.

He grunted. "More like you hadn't decided if you wanted to trust me yet. Never trust someone too clever too quickly, eh?"[60]

"Ha ha." I laughed nervously. "Right."

"This changes everything," Tessa was saying from across the room. She was hovering near the ceiling now, removing page after page of her plans. "All we have to do is get it and go!"

---

59 Never trust someone too clever too quickly.

60 Gah! I totally said that first! See? Clever people are so annoying...

"Not so fast," I said. I pointed at Tav, inviting him to speak.

"Draculadon are notoriously difficult to kill," Tav said.

"They're *impossible* to kill," Drake said. "The last remaining one died hundreds of years ago, and no one in living history claims to have seen one, let alone killed one."

"*Our* living history, Drake?" I said.

Drake smacked the side of his head. "Right. I guess I might not have the most up-to-date information." He looked around in horror. "I've been studying the wrong thing!"

"Don't worry about it, Drake," I said. "Tav here is an expert."

"Really?" Drake said suspiciously.

"No," Tav admitted. "But I know an expert. At least, I know the only person in *our* history to have defeated a draculadon."

"Who?" Tessa said.

"Xerith."

"Yeah, yeah," Tessa said. "If he's real. If we could find him."

"Oh, he's real, all right," Tav said. "My grandfather says he met him once—though I don't know if that's true. But I know where to find him."

Tessa's eyes went wide. She floated over to the wall and pulled down the picture with the question-mark face. "This is it, then. He might be able to tell us how to defeat the draculadon without killing it, and he might be able to convince you there's no way out of your situation in the tomb of Rone."

"You mean he might be able to *get* me out of my situation in the tomb of Rone," I said stubbornly.

"Whatever," Tessa said, turning back to Tav. "Where is he?"

He grinned. "Everyone knows."

"Uh, no," Tessa said. "We've been asking. *Nobody* knows."

"No," Tav said patiently. "*Everyone* knows. Nobody *says*. Nobody likes to think about it, because nobody who goes there comes back, usually." His expression went dark, as if he were remembering something painful, or trying not to. He shook himself. "He's in Sector 99."

"What?" Tessa said, looking at her map. "I thought Sector 99 was empty? They tried to build it—a special sector that reached to the heart of the planet—but it collapsed. It's supposed to be uninhabitable. Dangerous. They closed it off."

"Yeah," Tav said. "And that's where he lives. Doesn't want to be bothered, see?"

"Couldn't be worse than the Island of Yap. Or the Star of Dark Haven," I said brightly.

"I suppose…" Tessa said. She seemed anything but certain.

"That settles it, then," I said. "The four of us will go and find Xerith."

"No way," Tav said. "You three have fun. I'm not going anywhere near Sector 99."

"Seriously?" Drake said incredulously. "You go through all that trouble telling us it's the answer, and then you refuse to go?"

"Yeah," Tav said. "*I* don't want to die. Plus, it may be an answer, but it might not be the only one. I've heard rumors about Xerith. That he had some sort of special weapon, and that that's how he killed the draculadon."

"If that's true, don't you think Broca would have tried it?" I asked.

"Maybe not," Tav said. "It's just a rumor. And great wizards don't always think they need to follow in someone else's footsteps to succeed. They try to do it their own way. Even if he did try to find out the truth behind the rumors of Xerith's weapon, he wouldn't have had the resources that I do."

"Oh?" Tessa said. "And what resources are those?"

"My father was the king's weapons master. He knew everything there was to know about secret weapons. I'll figure out what he knows, and then I'll find the weapon and...borrow it."

"Steal it, you mean," I said.

"Whatever."

We stared at him for a while, each of us no doubt having the same thought: that it was a bad idea to let him go off gallivanting[61] alone now that he knew our plans. Maybe we had trusted him a bit too soon.

Drake sighed. "I'll go with Tav," he said.

"No, I'll go," I said. "You—"

---

61 *I'm* the only one who gets to gallivant in this story.

"No, Simon," Drake said. "You have questions to ask Xerith. You need to talk to him, not me. I'll go with Tav and try to keep him from doing anything stupid. No offense," he added to Tav.

Tav grinned. "None taken. You guys seem to be good people. I'm the guy who is trying to apprentice himself to the evil wizard, remember? I never pretended to be anything else." He offered us a wicked grin, and I couldn't decide if he was trying to be funny.

"Fine," Tessa said. "When do we start?"

"I don't know about the rest of you," Tav said, "but I've already wasted half a day. That leaves me one and a half days left. If you can figure out how to steal your magic necklace, you can have it. In the meantime, I'll be slaying the draculadon. Best of luck."

With that, he walked out of the room. And Drake, with one last worried look at me, ran out after him.

Tessa and I were left alone. I glanced at her levitating body shelf. "Are you…err, ready to go?"

She didn't answer.

I searched around for something nonchalant to say, hoping to keep her calm. "I noticed Drake's still licking the kulrakalakia. Still no luck, I take it. I would have thought he'd run out of the stuff by now."

Tessa snorted. "He's made two new batches since we've been here. Loni took him shopping for the ingredients. She likes him, I think."

"Yeah?" I said.

She grinned. "Yeah."

Unsure of what else to say, I tried something new, and I kept my mouth shut. And that's when a thing happened which had not happened for some time.

Leto climbed out of my boot.[62]

He stretched his tiny orange wings and soared around the room before landing on the glass near Tessa's navel. He leveled a serious look at me and said in his disproportionately deep voice, "We need to talk."

"Nice to see you too," I said. "How's my foot doing?"

"Simon, you *cannot* kill that draculadon. You know that, don't you?"

"I do," I said.

"Good." He licked a scaly arm like a cat. "Because if you did, I would have to kill *you*."

"I figured," I said.

"I don't want to kill you, Simon," Leto went on, as if he hadn't heard me. "Apart from being very dull, it would make the time I have invested in your journey a complete waste."

"Thanks," I said. "Of course, I still have to get the bloodstone."

"Of course," Leto said.

"And so, I might need to ask someone *how* to, err...

---

62 As you know, I have a dragon living in my boot. Just a miniature one, but still. If you've read the last two volumes of my autobiography, you will know that he is generally a silent, useless participant in my adventures and resides mostly in the *foot*notes. He's sort of the fire-breathing backseat driver of this series. He has his reasons for coming along for the ride, and he has a role to play later, so don't forget about him. I certainly can't. No, really, I have a permanent dent in my ankle.

defeat a draculadon, even though I don't intend to kill it.

"Hmm," Leto said, eyeing me critically. "Sometimes the mere possession of deadly force is enough to discourage violence. Is that your argument?"

"I don't know what that means," I said, "but Mr. Miyagi said Daniel-san had to learn how to fight so that he didn't have to fight."

"What?"

"Never mind. Did you have some sort of plan? Any ideas on how to proceed with the draculadon, or did you just want to threaten me?"

Leto arched his back haughtily. "I came to offer my services as a translator."

"Really?" I said, perking up. "I hadn't even considered talking to the draculadon."

"You most certainly cannot!" Leto flitted into the air and smacked me on the side of my nose. "It would be terribly rude for you to address the draculadon. They are the highest of all dragons, you know. Our predecessors. The ancient ones. The one that silly wizard has imprisoned is named Thestraelin. My mother sang 'Thestraelin's Lament' to me when I was a baby, and her mother sang it before her, and so on, back to the times when Thestraelin first sang the lament herself when her mother was destroyed by the folly of men."

"Ah," I said, feeling very confused. "So you know this Thestraelin?"

"I know *of* her. Have you ever heard of Adam and Eve?"

"Sure," I said.

"There you go."

"Who are Adam and Steve?" Tessa asked, looking confused.

"*Eve,*" I said. "Adam and—Never mind. Leto, if you're not going to translate for me, then what do you want to do?"

"Why, I wish to speak with her alone, of course."

"Oh," I said. "Right. I think I can arrange that."

"Good, then," Leto said. He flew back to the mouth of my boot and slithered inside. "And Simon?"

"Yeah?"

"You have an ingrown toenail."

13 THE BINDLE CAGE

Insanity is relative. It depends on who has who locked in what cage.

—Ray Bradbury[63]

Tessa and I made it back to Broca's lair without incident. Okay…there may have been *one* little incident when I pointed out that we couldn't just walk around outside with Tessa's top half glued to a floating slab of glass. Who wants that kind of attention? Judging by her reaction to my objection, I may not have phrased my words with enough sensitivity. Suffice it to say we had a bit of an argument, after which it was determined that I would simply transport her in the turncoat.

This solved more problems than one, because I had been worried about Broca meeting Tessa. If you're wondering what I did with Broca's sword when it popped out of the turncoat, I tried to convince Tessa to hold on to it, but she was still too miffed at me, so I stuck it down the back of my pants[64] instead, tucking the hilt beneath the hem of my coat.

63 An American author famous for his book *Fahrenheit 451*.
64 Very carefully.

As it happened, I didn't see Broca at all. I got all the way into the lab, through the trapdoor, and to the Groan without any problems. I opened it, and Leto hopped inside with such cool grace that you wouldn't know he was entering an inescapable prison. I let Leto through the trapdoor and into the Groan. I had to close the Groan, really, but I made a point of *not* locking the trapdoor on my way out. He told me to come back for him later if I had time. If not, he said, he would be fine. Dragons…

Broca stepped into the room with Sipher gliding along beside him just as I was replacing the rug.

GOODNESS. HAVE YOU KILLED TAV ALREADY, SIMON? I HAD RATHER EXPECTED IT TO BE THE OTHER WAY AROUND...

"He's still alive," I said. "We split up for a while."

I SEE...

Broca stopped several feet from me and cocked his head, sniffing the air.

BUT THEN WHO IS WITH YOU? YOU DON'T SEEM TO BE ALONE.

"Uh," I said, looking around. "Nobody here. Just me."

Broca frowned.

DON'T LIE TO ME.

The medallion in my forehead flashed red hot, and I found myself spilling the beans quite involuntarily: "There's a girl hidden in my coat."

HOW TYPICAL. GO ON, THEN. GET HER OUT.

My hand turned E8 (*Stash*), again unwillingly, and

Tessa popped into existence a few feet from me, floating in midair on her glass.

"Simon!" Tessa said. "It is so *weird* inside that coat. Let's make *you* go inside next time, okay? Simon, my glass isn't moving. I'm stuck!" She smacked her head. "Rats. I bet it doesn't locomote correctly when it gets too far from the space it was designed to work in. Oh…" she said, finally spotting Broca. "Oh, uh… Hello."[65]

WHO MIGHT THIS BE?
AND WHAT IS SHE DOING IN MY LAB?

I watched Tessa's upper half gyrate oddly as she tried to move her glass through the air, but it seemed stuck in place. I searched for something convincing to say. Something other than the truth, of course, because it's never safe to tell evil wizards the truth. "You have your slaves," I said cryptically, "and I have mine."

"I *beg* your pardon?" Tessa said and slapped me.

I stumbled backward, holding my face, and Sipher flitted wildly toward me, printing again.

I TRUST YOU HAVE NOT BEEN SHARING MY SECRETS WITH THIS GIRL. THE SECRETS WHICH I FORBADE YOU FROM REVEALING TO ANYONE…

The medallion went hot again, and I forced myself not to speak. I thought about turning B2 (*Silvertongue*) in the hope that I might say something really smooth to get me out of this situation, but fear had me second-guessing myself, so I put my hand in my pocket and touched the sorrowstone instead.

65 *Dang*, she talks a lot sometimes.

You remember that, don't you? It had been a parting gift from Gladstone on the day we boarded the *Calliope*. I think it was a major oversight that I had not used it more often, for the second I touched it, my fear vanished, replaced by absolute peace. From the void of that peace, I knew exactly what to do. I reached for—

Broca made a startled, moaning sound and leaped forward, grabbing at the hand in my pocket. He jerked it out and pried the sorrowstone from between my fingers.

"YOU'VE BEEN STEALING FROM ME!" he screamed. His face was contorted in rage, and I was actually afraid one of his eyes might pop out.[66]

"You can *talk*!" I said.

"Of course I can talk," he snapped. He waved a hand, and Sipher swooped out of the room. "What kind of wizard do you think I am, unable to heal myself from being deaf and dumb? When did you steal this from me? How?"

"Why do you pretend you can't talk?" I said, still reeling from this revelation.

"People say things around a deaf and dumb person that they would normally keep to themselves. Your conversation with Tav about the origin of my boots comes to mind. Now, when did you steal this from me, and how did you manage it?"

"I didn't," I said honestly. "If you have one too, it must be a coincidence."

"Lies," he said. "There is only *one* sorrowstone. I

66 This actually happens to little dogs (like Chihuahuas and Doxens) pretty often. Sad (kind of).

invented it. If this is a second, then how do you explain that mine is missi—"

He was patting the pocket of his shirt when he stopped talking. His brow furrowed as he pulled a second sorrowstone out of his pocket. It was identical to mine, right down to the small chip in the lower-left corner.

"I don't understand," he mumbled. "Unless…" He took a small knife out of a hidden pocket in his sleeve and made a deep scratch on the face of the stone he had pulled from his own pocket. As he did so, the scratch appeared on my stone, too. It was much fainter, but it was definitely there.

"Fascinating," he said. "This is the same stone."

"The same?" I said, trying to keep up.

"Goudy Old Style!" Tessa swore.

"Indeed. This *is* my sorrowstone." He held up the one from his own pocket. "And this is my sorrowstone, too. Hundreds of years older. *When* are you from, Simon?"

"I, uh…"

He held up a hand. "Wait. Don't tell me." He appeared agitated by some new thought. "Perhaps you are some enemy or pupil of mine from the future. You obviously don't possess the power to travel through time on your own, so I presume that I aided you. I must have. Otherwise why would you come to me? I must have sent you back. Did I?"

"Uh—"

"Wait!" he said, raising his other hand and running it through his hair frantically. "No! Don't tell me that, either.

Too dangerous to know. The future is a capricious mistress. Don't tell me. Don't tell me *anything*." He began to back away from me as if I were contagious. "I will continue my interactions with you as if this never happened. I will trust you to go about your business. If you harm me, I will destroy you. But I don't think you will. No. I think *I* sent you here. No! Don't tell me." He was practically running out of the room now.

"STOP!" I said in a commanding tone.

To my surprise, he did.

"I should give this back to you," I said. "I don't think I'll need it now." I drew his sword out of my pants and tossed it to him.

He caught it, looking confused. Then he pulled the copy from the scabbard at his side and inspected them both. Under his gaze, the copy burst into flame and then vanished. "How…?" he began, but stopped himself. "No. Never mind." He sheathed the real sword and backed away again. "A-anything you need?"

"How about a convenient way to transport my friend here? I don't think she likes riding in my coat, and I can't exactly run around with her like this."

He pointed to a small cage hanging from the back wall but offered no explanation. When I glanced back at him, he was gone. We were alone once more.

"What just happened?" Tessa said.

"Oh," I said, feeling somewhat smug, "I think I pretty well freaked out my evil slave master."

"And why did you give him back his sword?"

"To freak him out even more. He *definitely* doesn't know what to think of me now."

She shook her head. "I don't understand men."

The cage on the back wall didn't look like much. I had to climb up and get it while Tessa looked on from the middle of the room since she was no longer mobile. It was high up, and I had to stack about thirty books up into a makeshift ladder to reach it. I may or may not have fallen off that stack on my way down, scattering books everywhere.

"Are you going to pick those up?" Tessa said.

"Fat chance. What do you think this is?" The basket in my hands was really a small woven cage about the size of a softball. It hung from a slender chain, which was attached to a thin but sturdy stick, presumably so that a person could lay the stick across one shoulder and dangle the basket behind them for convenience, not unlike a bindle.[67]

"I'm not going to fit in there," Tessa said. "Do you think he was joking?"

"Broca may never have joked in his life," I said. "Stick your face in there or something and see what happens."

"My face?" Tessa said. "Are you kidding? I'll stick my finger in, thank you very much. I'd start with a toe, but then if I had my toes, we wouldn't need this stupid basket, would we?"

---

67 Also called a hobo stick, or a bindle stick. Typically created by tying a blanket or cloth to the end of a stick, thereby facilitating a more comfortable carry method for heavier loads. The word bindle is either (here we go again) a portmanteau of bind and spindle or else is derived from the German bündel, which means something tied and bound for carrying.

I stared at the ground shamefully, since that's what I thought she wanted me to do. Luckily I looked up just in time to see her stick her pinky finger in the little cage door.[68]

No sooner had she done so, she vanished. At least, that's what I thought at first. The bindle cage (that's what we're going to call it) swung wildly, and it was heavier than I remembered, nearly tugging itself out of my loose grip. I glanced around for Tessa and heard a very faint screaming.

"Bauhaus," I swore. "I've killed her *other* half. I can still hear the screams! At least we still have her legs. Somewhere…"

The screaming stopped. "You freak!" a tiny, high-pitched voice called. "I'm not dead. It worked! And what good would my legs do you anyway?"

I peered into the cage. Tessa looked unhurt, and exactly the same, except that she was quite a bit smaller.

"How tall do you think you are?" I said. "Two inches?"

She nestled against the bars of the bindle cage and gave me a scathing look.

"You know what?"

"Don't say it," she said, glaring.

"I bet you'd be *four* inches tall if you had legs."

68 Wouldn't it be hilarious if Tessa lost her pinky too? That could be our new thing: Every other book, someone loses a pinky. I mean… not funny, but, you know…dramatically ironic, or something… Okay… Tessa's giving me her "Stop writing stupid footnotes about me and get back to the story or you can cook dinner by yourself for the rest of your life" face. Seriously, girls have amazing expressions. By the way, how's that for foreshadowing?

"And I bet you'd look less like a half-digested pistachio nut if you had ears."

I couldn't help but laugh. "That hurts, Tessa."

"I feel ridiculous," Tessa said. "What am I supposed to do? Watch you from my tiny prison as you *carry* me around, doing stuff? How did we come to this?"

"You could read a book if you get bored," I said, picking up one of the fallen ones, a small, leather-bound one with a red cover, and shoving it into the cage. To my delight the book shrank in size and toppled to the floor of the cage beside her.

"You're an idiot, Simon," Tessa said, shaking her head. "Come on. Let's get out of here."

"Right," I said, sweeping out of the room and up the stairs. "Off to search the abandoned, dangerous, uninhabited sector of Tarinea for a mysterious recluse who lives there because he doesn't want to be bothered and will probably kill us or grind our bones to make tortillas after he answers our questions. If he answers them at all…"

"You're a little insane, Simon."

"Thanks."

"You know normal people don't talk like that, right?"

"I know."

"Seriously. If your life ends up being made into a movie or a book or something, that line is going to sound just silly."

"I know."

"Simon?"

"What?"

"Drop me and I'll *kill* you."

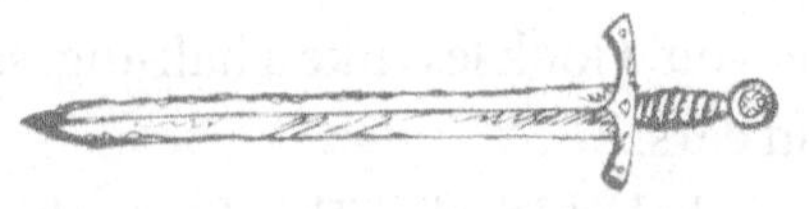

"Are you sure this is the right place?"

Tessa and I were looking at the ramshackle bones of what may have once been an outhouse. It stood several yards from the very last house in a long line of white stone houses at the edge of the residential quarter.

"I'm sure," Tessa said. "I read about it."

"Exactly how much did you read about this place?" I said.

"Most of what's written actually. The problem is, that isn't very much. No one seems to know about this place. Or care. The few people who have gone looking for answers haven't returned."

"Lovely."

I pressed the latch, which happened to be one of the only parts of the tiny building that was still in good repair, and pushed the door open.

Tessa gasped.

"Well, that's unsettling," I said.

Of course, when you open the door to any sort of building, you expect to see the inside. Not so in this case. There was nothing inside. And I mean nothing. No light. No sound. No movement of air to suggest the existence of something beyond what we could see.

"Well," Tessa said. "This looks promising."

"That's what I like about you, Tessa. You're always so positive."

I adjusted the bindle cage on my shoulder and stepped into the abyss.

Evil is unspectacular, and always human, and shares our bed and eats at our table.

—W. H. Auden[69]

One of the limitations of writing a book in first person is that I can only tell the story from one perspective: mine. This is a fairly firm rule (firmer if you have set a precedent in the last two books, like I have), one that only idiots, first-year English majors, and extremely brilliant writers ever break. Of course, we are getting pretty good at breaking literary laws by now. And so:

Drake had to run now and then to keep up with Tav's longer strides. He must have looked silly, an ancient minotaur (he had donned his disguise before leaving Grandma Loki's) galloping at the heels of a young wizard.

They booked it out of Sector 42, and Tav walked briskly down the row of white stone houses in the residential quarter. Drake was still a pace or two behind as Tav rounded a corner and cut across the path to a different neighborhood.

---

69 An English poet. He coined the phrase "The Age of Anxiety" and won a Pulitzer Prize for a poem of the same name.

"Why do you keep licking that green slime ball?" Tav said without turning around. "The others don't seem to notice, but that's the third or fourth time I've seen you at it."

Drake stuffed the kulrakalakia back into his pants pocket. "Special minotaur snack," he lied. "I take some when I'm nervous, I guess."

"If you say so," Tav said. He approached a house which, despite being superficially identical to the other manicured stone houses, nevertheless felt somehow dilapidated. The little green plants beside the door drooped. The white stone was a shade darker. The door had not been painted as recently.

Tav opened it, and Drake followed him into a dank and dreary swampland. The door shut behind them, and Drake had to shield his eyes while they adjusted to the diminished light of the swamp.

A second after they arrived, Drake gagged and doubled over.

"Unique smell, isn't it?" Tav said.

"Ugh. I've met newborn yukawyrms that smell better. Who would choose to live here?"

"Exactly who you'd expect," Tav said. "I grew up here, back before Father worked for the king. Now my grandfather works out of here because fewer people come to call."

"I believe it," Drake said. He was standing on a riverbank, his boots slowly sinking into the soft earth. He pulled them out with a squelching noise and took a half step to the right, where he immediately began to sink again.

"Not a good place to stand around," Tav said.

"So I gathered. Where are we headed?"

"See those lights?"

Drake saw them. He also saw the rickety, half-dilapidated wooden walkways suspended over the river and swamp. They looked liable to fall apart if you stepped wrong.

"Careful," Tav said, mounting the nearest walkway and moving forward cautiously. "They're liable to fall apart if you step wrong."

"Lovely." Drake squelched over to the boards and pulled himself up. At least it would be better than swimming through the swamp.

It didn't take as long as Drake thought to reach the lights. They turned out to be lanterns. In the center of the swamp was a series of piers with little wooden boats moored in row after row. Boat was a stretch, really—they were more like rafts. Rafts with tall edges and a tentlike structure in the middle, where presumably the boat's occupants could take refuge from the swamp. Each boat had its own lantern hanging from a pole on one end, attracting all sorts of bugs. "What's with the lights?"

"They scare off the swamp weasels."

"Swamp weasels?"

"Don't worry," Tav said, stepping off the pier and onto a particularly shabby-looking raft. "We're here." The tent flap was stained from top to bottom as if someone had thrown out the garbage and missed. Tav ducked inside, and after a moment's hesitation, Drake followed.

Drake gasped as the tent flap closed behind him. The sound of that gasp echoed across a massive chamber. It was a library of sorts, though larger than any hall he had seen even at Skelligard. Unique in its construction was a floor of polished blue stone, like lapis lazuli, and into the stone was set a myriad of bright golden stars, mimicking the night sky outside. They swirled and moved about from time to time, set to some internal clock that differed from the real world.

The room was so large that it would have taken Drake several seconds to sprint across it. Bookshelves rose from floor to ceiling, and here and there polished wooden ladders leaned against the high shelves. On the far end of the room, surrounded by stacks and stacks of books piled on the floor, an old man with spectacles sat reading at a desk.

Tav approached the man, his soft boots echoing loudly in the still chamber. "Grandfather," he said when he was in front of the desk.

"Mmm?" The old man peered out over his spectacles with unfocused eyes, his thoughts still elsewhere.

"I came for an audience with Father."

"Mmm." He looked back down at his book, lifted a pen, and noted something in the margin.

"Good talk," Tav said. Tav circled around to the other side of the desk and moved toward a small door in the back wall.

The old man cleared his throat, and Tav stopped.

"Where is your brother?"

"Don't know," Tav said. "Don't care."

"Mmm."

Tav raised his eyebrows at Drake from behind the old man's back and pushed the little door open.

On the other side, a sparsely furnished room looked out onto the swamp water through a small round window set high in the wall. The room was cramped, entirely unlike the previous chamber, and held only a single chair and a small stone box.

Tav sat in the chair and slid the lid off the box, lifting out a round, pale white object.

"That's a skull," Drake said sharply. "Tav, is that…"

"Dear old dad," Tav said, replacing the lid on the box. He struck a match then and set it squarely in the center of the stone so that the small flame flickered, casting shadows across the walls. Then he set the skull on top of the match.

Drake sneezed. "Courier New, Tav!" Drake swore. "I've read about this. Are you contacting the dead? This is dark magic. Dark, *dark* magic."

"It's not so bad," Tav said. "My father did a deal with someone he shouldn't have. Grandfather's been trying to bring him back—that's why he brought us back here—but he's never going to succeed. You can't bring back the dead." Tav sighed. "Anyway, this is how we have to talk with Father now. Not very convenient, but there you go."

Smoke was twisting out of the eye and nasal sockets now, forming into an amorphous cloud just below the ceiling. The fire flashed inside the skull, lighting it up from within, and a face formed in the cloud above.

"Hello, Father," Tav said. "How's the underworld?"

The face twisted in distaste. "Where is your brother?" it asked in a gravelly voice.

Tav's expression twisted in anger. "Don't know," he said. "Don't care. *I'm* here, Father, and I need your help."

"You have a way to set me free?"

Tav hesitated. "Grandfather is still working on that. This is something else. I need your help finding a weapon."

"A weapon?"

"Perhaps from the king's collection. Do you know anything about the weapon Xerith used to slay the draculadon?"

"Xerith?" The smoke head huffed. "Never met him. Just a legend. Of course, everyone knows—or at least they once did—that he slayed that beast with a spear from Tilanar. The Spear of Eternity, we labeled it. Had it on display for decades, you know. Sent it back to the royal armory when we closed the exhibit. Just a legend, though, like I said. Probably not even real."

"Grandfather says Xerith is real."

"My father is a liar and a cheat! Lazy. Don't talk to me about him until he has a plan to get me out of this place."

"Is the spear still there?" Tav asked.

"How should I know?"

Tav tossed his father's skull back in the box and slammed the lid shut.

Drake coughed as the smoke dissipated.

"Well," Tav said, "there you go, Drake. The Spear of Eternity. And it's in the royal armory. Perfect. I've always wanted to break in there. You up for it?"

"Uh," Drake said, stifling a sneeze. "Is there any way we could just ask to borrow the spear or something?"

"Sure, Drake," Tav said. "We'll try that first. *Then* we'll steal it. And Drake, don't tell anyone what you saw here, okay? You know, people in this day and age don't look kindly on talking with the dead."

"People don't like it in any day and age. When I come from, it's illegal to even write or teach about magic like this."

"Ah," Tav said. "Yes, well… Desperate times call for desperate measures."

"Right." Drake was feeling less and less comfortable around his new companion.

"You don't have to come, you know," Tav said. "But if you do, stay out of my way." With that, Tav exited the little room, leaving Drake alone.

For a second, Drake considered his options. Sure, he had told Simon that he would help Tav. Keep an eye on him. Sure, it might even be important to get that spear, especially if Simon failed to find a way to defeat the draculadon without killing it. But anyone that communicated with the dead could *not* be trusted. It wasn't wise.

It wasn't safe.

Not that it made a difference. It wasn't like he could go back now. And anyway, he'd given up on things like wisdom and safety the moment he became Simon's friend, hadn't he? Drake gritted his teeth, tightened his belt, and took a lick of the kulrakalakia. As usual, nothing happened. He was beginning to think he was destined to be frail and weak forever. Oh well. "Wait for me!" he called, and ran through the door after Tav.

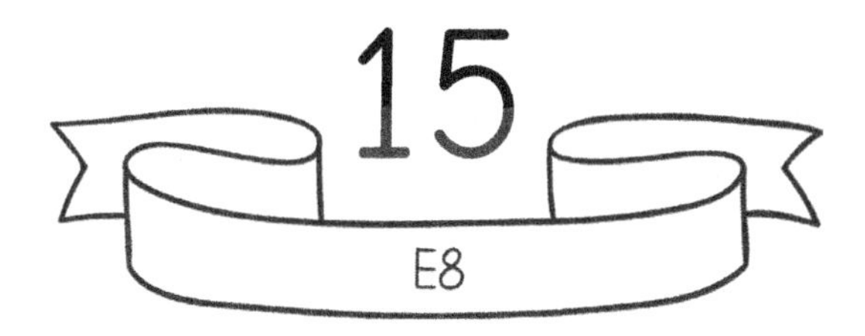

A woman is like a tea bag—you can't tell how strong she is until you put her in hot water.

—Eleanor Roosevelt[70]

Tessa and I never landed. We just sort of…appeared. It took a while for me to figure out why the air was so thick. Then I tried to breathe and nearly died.

We were underwater.

Have I mentioned it was an *unlucky* day?

I thrashed frantically, clawing for the surface. I never got there. I nearly dropped the bindle cage in my panic. The thing that saved me was that I realized I was completely out of my depth (excuse the pun)[71]. I truly had no idea what to do. Death was mere seconds away.

I opened the coat, turned A7 (*Epiphany*), and had an epiphany: There was nowhere for me to go. Now, that may

---

70 Niece of U.S. President Theodore Roosevelt, and wife to U.S. President Franklin D. Roosevelt. She urged her husband to stay in politics after he was confined to a wheelchair. Later, while serving as first lady, she played a major role in running the country and changing the nation's perceptions of women in the 1920s.

71 My editor would like you to know that this is not actually a pun. It's an idiom. Wait… No… Now she says it's both.

seem obvious to you, but in my experience, it is actually very difficult to see the obvious truth when you are stuck dead center in a high-stress situation.

Here is what I realized: I could have been twenty or thirty feet underwater (or a hundred), and I didn't know which way was up. I had to escape somewhere, and although I assumed there was nowhere to go, it turned out there was. I shifted my hand, opened the pocket of E8 (*Stash*), stuck my finger inside, and turned the knob.

Several people have been inside the turncoat pocket by now. When I asked them later what it was like, they described a dark room with no walls.

That is NOT what it was like for me. For a minute, I was certain that I had somehow turned the wrong knob—perhaps a knob that I had never turned before—and had been transported directly back to our clearing in Fluff. But it wasn't really Fluff. The clearing was there. And the tentreecles waving gradually in a wind that didn't exist, and our beds were there. And the table. The sky, as well as the space between the grove of tentreecles that surrounded us, were not natural.

"Quick thinking, Simon." Tessa's voice choked as she coughed water onto the floor of the now sopping-wet bindle cage. I jumped at the sound of it. "Why am I still tiny?" she asked.

"Don't know. At least the turncoat let you inside! I wasn't sure it would, to be honest. More than one person, and all that, you know. Maybe it let you in because, you know, being cut in half, lost in time, and miniaturized, you're more of an object than a person."

Tessa groaned, wringing out her shirt into a tiny puddle on the floor of the cage. "Didn't your mother ever tell you it's not polite to objectify women?"

"Is this what the turncoat pocket is like inside all the time?"

"Not even close," Tessa said. "Usually it's dark, and you can't see outside at all."

She was right. I realized as she said it that the swirling dark stuff I was looking at through the tentreecles and in the sky was actually the water we had just been in outside. It was like some sort of weird 360-degree cosmic window.

Tessa stuck her arm out of the cage and reappeared at her normal size. Her levitating glass did not seem to work at all inside the turncoat, however, and it simply rested upon the ground. That was all right with Tessa, since the ground was warm, just like it was on the real Fluff. Tessa shivered, wringing out her hair some more. The water had been cold. Why hadn't I realized that? Clearly my mind was number than my body.[72]

72 As they say in the cold places of the world, "the number you get, the dumber you get." By the way, *number* is another homonym. I was using the word as an adjective. Like, "It's so cold I'm numb! My fingers are number than my toes!" Not like the noun: "I'm missing a pinky! I have a different number of fingers than toes!) This, of course, gives me the opportunity to lecture you again about this dark and twisted slippery slope of the English language: Homonyms. If you remember, they are words that sound the same, but mean something different and may or may not be spelled the same. A subgroup of homonyms called homophones are words that are spelled differently (like pear and pair). On the other side of the fence, you have homographs. These are words that are *spelled* the same but mean something different

and may or may not *sound* the same. A subcategory of homographs are heteronyms; these words are always spelled the same, but never sound the same (*tear* on your cheek, *tear* in a piece of fabric). As you can see, homographs can also be homonyms, but only if they sound the same. Likewise, homonyms are also homographs, but only if they are spelled the same. Of course, heteronyms are never homonyms but always homographs, while homophones are always homonyms but never heteronyms, and giraffes are never koala bears but always quadrupeds. Now, as a tribute to geeky and torturous English teachers everywhere, I have included for you a list of words. For extra credit, decide which of these words (and their relatives) are homonyms, homographs, homophones, and heteronyms. The most interesting thing to me is that words are often pronounced differently (but spelled the same) when they are being used as nouns instead of verbs, and so forth. I hope that you are shocked and appalled by how many words there are with different spellings, different sounds, multiple meanings, etc. No wonder Eengwish is hawd to wuhn: accent, attribute, axes, bass, bat, bow, buffet, bustier, compact, compound, content, contract, coordinates, desert, dessert, digest, discount, does, entrance, moped, object, proceeds, project, putting, refuse, read, reed, red, read, row, second, subject, wind, wound, break, brake, cell, sell, cent, scent, flour, flower, for, four, heal, heel, hear, here, hour, our, idle, idol, knight, night, knot, not, pour, poor, right, write, sea, see, sole, soul, son, sun, nun, none, steal, steel, tail, tale, weather, whether, accept, except, affect, effect, compliment, complement, then, than, to, too, you're, your. P.S. This mess is one of the seven primary reasons for the existence of editors and proofreaders: it's their—not *there,* mind you—job to know whether you mean *compliment*, as in to say something nice, or *complement*, as in to enhance the inherent attributes of something. Wait...did I get those backwards? And did you stumble over the word *attributes* just now? As a funny aside, I went through (not *threw*) most of my life falsely believing that *settence* (a group of words containing a subject and a predicate) and *sentence* (the punishment assigned by a judge) were two different words that illiterate people commonly mispronounce and confuse with each other. Joke's on me, though, because *settence* isn't the correct spelling of any word at all, and both words are spelled (and pronounced) *sentence.* Turns out *I* was the

Tessa reached into the bindle cage and pulled out what looked like a tiny red postage stamp, which instantly sprang back to its normal size. "Gah," she said. "You got my book all wet."

"How long do you think this is going to take?" I said, looking at the swirling darkness outside.

"I don't know."

"Assuming we are in some body of water, we should eventually float to the top, right? Leather floats… Right?"

"Sure… I think so." She was peeling the pages of the book apart, letting them begin to dry out.

I sighed. "We might be in here for a long time."

"Good thing we brought some reading material," she said brightly. She was examining the cover now. *Mechanics of the Mind* by…hmm…looks like Broca wrote it himself, actually.

"What?"

"I said it looks like Broca—"

"You're kidding!" I said, snatching the book out of

---

illiterate one the whole time. How embarrassing is that? A writer who doesn't know (not *no*) what a sentence is. P.P.S. If you seriously read (not red, reed, or read) *this* far into a footnote this boring and absurd, you must be a true fan. I hereby reward your truefanness by giving you this spoiler (spoiler alert!): The Tike dies in Book 5. Sort of. Actually, the whole universe dies in Book 5. Sort of. Except for me, of course (duh). Sort of. Book 5 is going to be crazy… You will be happy to learn that the final pages of the final book have already been written and (for safekeeping) downloaded onto a flash drive and hidden inside a hollow playpen ball in a bouncy house in a Chuck-E-Cheese in an undisclosed state (starts with an N). Of course, being a superfan, you probably want to go looking for it, so I'll give you a hint: the ball is red. Red red read red!

her hands and studying the title. "I totally forgot. I know someone who would give anything to get their hands on this!"

"What are you talking about, Simon?"

"Gladstone," I said, laughing. "He was telling me about this book and how he really needed to read it but couldn't find a copy."

"Wonderful," Tessa said, sounding less than impressed. "You can bring him a souvenir, provided we don't die in here, or you know, *fail* at saving the universe. Student of the year. Mr. Wonderful, could you prop me up against something?"

"Huh?"

"My waist is glued to a piece of glass, genius. I noticed you are leaning up against your bed. See how I can't lean at all? See how I can't lay down? See how I have to just have good posture and stand upright? See how this is all your fault and you should stop questioning me and just do what I ask and give my book back?"

I did see, and I hurried to comply.

Luckily the bed had appeared complete with pillows, and I was able to prop them behind her so that she could lean against the table leg.

"Too bad we don't have any blankets," I said, noticing how she still shivered.

At once, a stack of thick woolen blankets appeared on the floor next to me. At the same time, I felt something flutter deep in my gut.

"Whoa," I said.

"Whoa," Tessa agreed, staring at the blankets.

I grabbed one and wrapped it around her shoulders.

"Simon," Tessa said slowly, "say there is a bowl of strawberries."

"There is a bowl of strawberries."

I felt the flutter deep in my gut again, and a large glass bowl appeared on the floor next to my knee, chock full of strawberries.

"Dang!" I said. "Tessa, I can make strawberries!"

Tessa, who had grabbed the bowl and was shoving several strawberries in her mouth, rolled her eyes at me and said (around a great deal of chewing), "Simon, I think you might be able to do anything in here." She shivered again, set down the strawberries, and continued to wring out her shirt. Then she stopped, eyes gleaming. "Simon! Say that I'm wearing a brand-new dry top."

"Tessa, you're wearing a brand-new dry top."

Tessa's wet shirt vanished, instantly replaced by what can only be described as a very minimalist hot-pink bikini top.

"SIMON!" Tessa shouted, wrapping the blanket around herself as I turned bright red.

"Oh, geez… Sorry!"

"SAY THAT I'M WEARING A *THICK*, WARM BROWN LONGSLEEVED CREWNECK SWEATER!"

I repeated her words exactly, making sure that as I did so I thought of nothing but thick ugly sweaters. To our relief, she was thereafter fully covered.

Tessa glared at me for a minute as I carefully examined

my fingernails. "Is there anything you want to say to me?" she said.

"Um… When that happened, I felt something… You know… Twitch in my uh…seat of power. I think I was actually doing real magic!"

Tessa rolled her eyes. "That's…not exactly what I meant. Still, I suppose that *is* more important. Simon, I think you're right. You *are* doing real magic in here."

"It makes sense," I said, eager to be moving on to a new subject. "If the turncoat is functioning as my channeling vessel like Drake said, then it makes sense that since I'm actually *inside* my channeling vessel, my magic flows perfectly."

"But…" she said, "that doesn't explain *how* you are able to do these things. I mean, making blankets is one thing, but creating food out of nothing is extremely complicated magic. How can you do it if you don't know *how* to do it?"

I shrugged. "I usually don't know what I'm doing in life. Why should this be any different?"

"It just *is*."

We sat for a while, pondering the implications of this new revelation. Outside, the blackness swirled on. There were no glimpses of distant light. No bubbles in the water. Nothing to suggest that we were nearing the surface. I thought about what I wanted to conjure next, what great magic I wanted to try now that I could apparently do anything.

Tessa ate strawberries, lost in her own thoughts.

I tried thinking something this time, rather than

saying it out loud, and a cheerful campfire crackled into being a few feet away. Tessa's eyes widened, and I flashed her a grin. She bit her lip thoughtfully and pulled the blanket tighter around her shoulders.

"Simon," she said, "do we need to have a discussion about what you are and are not allowed to think?"

"Nope."

"Good." Tessa ate another strawberry, and I tried very hard not think of anything in particular. More accurately, I tried not think of anything at all. The last thing I wanted to do was start thinking about something *random* but nonetheless unpleasant, like giant Yap rabbits or something. The one thing that gave me solace was that it seemed like I had to *will* my magic into action, not just think of it.

"SIMON!"

Then again, maybe not. Several giant Yap rabbits had appeared behind me and were staring at Tessa curiously, eyeing her strawberries. I focused my thoughts once more, and they disappeared.

"Okay," Tessa said breathlessly. "Okay." Her eye was twitching, the way it always did right before I accidentally destroyed the world. If she had feet, she no doubt would have risen to them. As it was, all she could do was wag a finger in my face. "I would like you to go to sleep now, Simon. Okay? Just go to sleep for a little while, and when I have a plan, I will wake you up. I think that's better than you just… You know…"

"Accidentally magicking us into oblivion?"

"Exactly," she said, breathing a sigh of relief. "You have a knob, remember? That puts you to sleep."

"I know. A5. Problem is, it's a *turncoat* knob, and if you haven't noticed, I'm not *wearing* the turncoat. We are *in* the turncoat."

"Right. I know. But I bet if you just say something like, 'I want to fall asleep now,' that would work just as well."

"A *dreamless* sleep?"

Her eyebrows rose. "Definitely."

I sighed. "All right. I want to fall into a dreamless sleep now and wake up whenever Tessa wants me to wake up."

And so I did.

16 LIPS AND DAGGERS

The sunlight claps the earth, and the moonbeams kiss the sea:
what are all these kissings worth, if thou kiss not me?

—Percy Bysshe Shelley[73]

Diamar, King of Tarinea, lived with his daughter, Princess Hiamene, in Sector 1 of Tarinea, in a castle of glowing blue stone built on the side of a mountain, surrounded by a lake of deadly fire. This Drake learned from Tav as they ran toward it.

"How are we going to get in?" Drake said.

"Not sure. Never been in!" Tav said as they rounded the last corner that stood between them and the house through which Sector 1 was accessed. "There it is, at the end of the street."

"Doesn't it have any guards?" Drake asked.

"Nope. Just the lake. It's enchanted. I guess they figure if you can get past that, then you deserve to be in the castle."

They paused at the door, and Tav opened it slowly,

73 An English poet who, though known today, was not at all famous in his lifetime. Even today, he is perhaps *most* famous for being married to Mary Shelley, who wrote the famous novel *Frankenstein*.

peering inside. "Looks like the coast is clear. No guards, as usual. Just the lake and the boats. Come on."

Tav disappeared through the door, and Drake followed, stifling a sneeze. He wished for about the fourteenth time that day that he'd had more time to prepare, to learn, to test his abilities, before coming on this quest. He felt constantly as if the world was on the brink of destruction, and there was nothing he could do about it.

They stepped out onto a rocky beach beneath a dark, starlit sky. Tall stone pillars stood here and there on the beach. A lake stood before them, its calm black water glinting with reflected starlight.

In the center of the lake stood a mountain, tall and strong, the right half of which was covered with the glowing blue walls and towers and gates of a giant castle. Light glinted from windows in the distance, a thousand points of light, and Drake found himself thinking what a silly idea this whole thing was.

"And just how are we supposed to find the armory inside *that* thing? And are you sure we have to steal this spear thing? Simon might still find a way to, you know, get what we need *without* killing the draculadon."

"I don't care what Simon needs, Drake," Tav said. "I can't get what *I* need without killing the draculadon. *I* need Broca to take me on as an apprentice, and *he* says to kill the draculadon, so that's what I'm going to do. If Simon gets his stone thingy, fine. Just so long as he doesn't get in my way."

Tav was staring at the castle with a hungry expression.

Then he broke away, giving Drake a smile. "But that doesn't matter. First thing's first, my hairy friend. The problem at hand is how to get to those boats. You do still want to come, I take it? I mean, you can always turn back. It's not like I invited you."

Drake gulped. "I…told Simon I would help you."

"*Watch* me is more like it. So what'll it be? You coming or not?"

Drake sighed. He could hardly let Tav go gallivanting off on his own. He might hurt someone. And then there was still the possibility that Tav was right, and they really *did* need the spear in order to get the bloodstone. "You say there are boats?"

Tav grinned. "Atta boy." He pointed at the lake, and for the first time Drake noticed that several dark, graceful boats floated thirty or forty feet from the shore. They were long and sleek, with upturned ends.

"Right," Drake said. "Didn't you say this was supposed to be a lake of fire?"

Tav picked up a rock from the shore and tossed it into the lake. When the stone touched the water, it burst into flame, spewing drops of lava into the air.

"Right," Drake said. "So, no swimming to the boats."

"Nope," Tav agreed.

"And I don't suppose you can jump thirty feet?"

"No," Tav said. "I mean, with the help of magic, but I've heard magic doesn't work on the lake. That's the point. Wizard security at its best, you know. The good thing is that since the castle is so safe because of the lake, there's not much security in the castle itself, which should make the second phase of our venture much easier."

"Assuming we ever make it through the first," Drake said.

"Right."

"And just what are you boys up to?"

A thin, willowy girl stepped out from behind one of the tall standing stones and crossed over to us, white hair glinting in the starlight.

"Loni!" Drake cried. "What are you doing here?"

"I followed you," she said simply. "Wondered where you were going. Thought you might need some help." She said this last bit shyly, putting her hands in her pockets.

"Do we ever!" Drake said. "You're apprenticed in the castle, right? With your grandmother? You must know how to get across the lake."

"Sure," she said. "It's easy. But it only works if you have business in the castle. Do you have business in the castle?"

"You bet we do," Tav said.

"*Legitimate* business?"

"Uh, no," Drake said.

"Then I'm afraid the boats won't let you cross. They only allow access to people with legitimate business who don't pose a threat to the castle."

Tav scowled. "I've never actually been across," he admitted. "I was hoping we could just, you know…"

"Force your way in?" Loni said. "It doesn't work like that."

"So what do you suggest?" Drake said.

"I suggest that you don't steal from the king," Loni said. "He's kind of my boss, you know. That *is* what you're planning, right? I couldn't help overhearing you earlier..."

"Wonderful!" Tav said. "Just like that I have another accomplice." He didn't seem very pleased. "I assume you're going to try to talk me out of robbing the armory as well?"

She turned to Drake. "Why are *you* going along? Do you and your friends need this thing that badly?"

Drake sighed. "Unfortunately, we might. I wouldn't—I mean. I don't... Well, the truth is the fate of the *universe* is kind of at stake."

"I believe you," she said.

Tav rolled his eyes. "How *romantic*."[74]

Drake blushed awkwardly. Then he sort of half-sneezed. Which means that he started to sneeze, then tried to stop himself.[75] By so doing he made a sound like a sick donkey and blew a jet of mucus out of one nostril.

Loni giggled. "Are you okay?" she said, handing Drake a handkerchief.

"*Geez*," Tav said. "Are you going to help us, or not?"

---

74 There are bits and pieces in here that, I'll be honest, I'm just guessing at. I mean, I wasn't there, and while I think we can trust Drake's account for most of what happened, we need to add flavor back in at certain places. For instance, Drake insists that there was no awkward blushing or sneezing at *all* during this exchange. But let's be honest. You and I both know that isn't possible. It's Drake!

75 *Never* try to stop a sneeze. The average sneeze moves air at over a hundred miles per hour and sends bits of mucus flying up to thirty feet. Does it *sound* like a good idea to stop something traveling at a hundred miles per hour using only your mouth? I think not. People have been known to literally rupture their throats trying. Luckily Drake survived this particular mistake.

Loni cleared her throat. "Well, since you asked so nicely, here." She took a thin knife out of her pocket and handed it to Tav, hilt first. It was at least four inches long and looked wickedly sharp. "Stab Drake in the stomach." She indicated a place just above Drake's navel. "Right here."

"What?" Drake squeaked.

"Nice and deep," she told Tav calmly. "Don't miss."

"Fine," he said, and he stabbed Drake hard in the gut.

Let us step into the night and pursue that flighty temptress, adventure.

—Albus Dumbledore[76]

I woke suddenly to the sight of Tessa pressing her finger gently against her lips.

Tessa was really pretty by the way.[77] Have I ever mentioned that? I bring it up not because this is going to turn into some kind of sappy, unrealistic romance novel where thirteen-year-olds start falling in love with each other but because it had just been on my mind a lot lately. At this particular moment, her hair was braided much the same as it had been the day I met her. Her eyes were the best part: one of them a frothy blue, the other a rich and vibrant brow—

"Simon, are you even listening to me?"

76 "Considered by many the greatest wizard of modern times, Dumbledore is particularly famous for his defeat of the Dark Wizard Grindelwald in 1945, for the discovery of the twelve uses of dragon's blood, and his work on alchemy with his partner, Nicolas Flamel. Professor Dumbledore enjoys chamber music and ten-pin bowling." —J.K. Rowling

77 "What do you mean I *was* pretty? I still *am* pretty. As far as *you're* concerned, I get prettier and prettier every day!!!!" —Tessa

"What?"

"Repeat after me, Simon: I command this to be law for as long as I stay inside the turncoat: that no magic will move from conception to reality without me saying the word 'peanut.'"

"Peanut?"

"REPEAT AFTER ME, SIMO—"

"I command this to be law for as long as I stay inside the turncoat: that no magic will move from conception to reality without me saying the word 'peanut.'"

"Perfect," she said. "Now try it out."

"I want a box of Hot Tamales," I said.

Nothing happened.

Tessa grinned.

"I want a box of Hot Tamales. *Peanut*," I said.

They appeared in my hand.

Tessa clapped jubilantly. Then she stole my Hot Tamales, opened the box, and popped several into her mouth. "What are these? Ooh, they're HOT!"

"Rat poison," I said.

She spat them out, then punched me.

"Well," I said when I had recovered, "what now?"

She was fishing the last strawberry out of the bowl (apparently she had been busy while I was asleep). "I dunno. *You're* the genius. If it was up to me, we'd play a few more games of 'repeat after me.'"

"Yeah, right. You just try to get me to say something like 'my nose is as big as a hippo and weighs 500 pounds.' Peanu—"

Luckily, I stopped myself before I finished that sentence.

Tessa give me a wicked grin.

I cleared my throat, inspecting the unchanged swirling blackness outside. "I want to be instantly transported to wherever Xerith is. Peanut."

Nothing happened.

"Yeah," Tessa said, "I thought about that, but I don't think you're going to have power to affect the outside world."

"Bummer. Maybe I should go back outside. I could leave you in here, try to swim for a while, and maybe—"

"No!"

"Fine, then. What can we do from in here?"

Tessa didn't respond.

I found myself looking at the red leather book that she was still holding.

"Hey… I want that book to be dried and fixed, like it never got wet in the first place. Peanut."

It was done.

"Hey," Tessa said, grinning. "That was very thoughtful of you."

"I try."

"Of course, it will just get wet again when we leave here, assuming we have to go through that water."

I grinned. "I want a special magic storage box to put that book in so that when we leave it will stay in the turncoat. Peanut."

A shoebox appeared in my lap, and I dropped the

book inside it, winking at Tessa. "Easy peasy."

"Okay, hot shot," Tessa said. "You've saved my *book*. Now what are we going to do?"

"Hmm..." I said, looking around thoughtfully. "I would like a map and a list of step-by-step instructions telling me exactly how to get from here to where Xerith is. Peanut."

Tessa raised her eyebrows.

Nothing happened.

"BankGothic MD!" I swore.

"Watch your language, mister."

"Sorry."

"You probably can't make that happen because it's outside of your understanding."

"And making strawberries appear out of thin air is inside my understanding?"

She shrugged. "You understand strawberries. You don't understand where Xerith is. In fact, you don't understand Xerith, so you probably won't be able to do anything with him."

I mulled that over for a while and ended up ordering Tessa a footlong meatball sub, an apple pie, and a bowl of ice cream, which she began to devour with relish.[78] "Why are you so hungry?"

"Grandma Loki's chicken was weird, okay? I couldn't eat it."

"Do you think I could magically transport Hawk here? Or the Tike?"

78 By which I mean, she ate it eagerly. No pickles were harmed in the making of this sandwich.

She shook her head. "Too risky. We don't really know how this whole time-travel thing works. It seems kind of messy to transport someone from where they are magically frozen in time, *through* time, into a half-finished section of Tarinea, to the inside of a magical object as powerful as the turncoat."

"Well, when you put it *that* way..." I mumbled. I thought for a while. It seemed ridiculous to sit here doing nothing, just waiting for the turncoat to float to the surface outside.

The turncoat... Something about that thought tickled in my mind. "You said I have to have an understanding of things before I can work magic with them, right?"

She nodded, unwrapping the second half of her Subway sandwich. "I think so. We're just guessing about all this, of course. This is *really* good, by the way. We have to get one of these Subway things at Skelligard."

"What if I am not necessarily the one who has to understand things for the magic to work? What if it just has to be understood?"

"You're saying you could do magic with something that I understand but you don't?" Tessa asked, looking confused.

"I'm saying I could do magic with something that I don't understand, but that the *turncoat* understands. I mean, the turncoat understands *itself*, right?"

"I guess," Tessa said. "What does that have to do with—Oh!"

"See what I mean?" I cleared my throat. "I would like a

detailed explanation of the function of all of the turncoat knobs on a piece of paper that appears in my hand. Peanut."

Nothing happened.

I sighed. "I would like *Tessa's* diagram explaining the function of the turncoat knobs to be completed and appear in my hand. Peanut."

Again, nothing happened.

Tessa made a face. "With the second one, you couldn't possibly understand something that I do in the future. That is, labeling the turncoat knobs. Still, I'm not sure why the first one didn't work..."

I grunted. I only had one more idea. "I would like a copy of Rellik's turncoat diagram—if he had one—as it looked before he died. Peanut."

A square piece of stained parchment appeared in midair beside me and glided to rest on the floor.

"Holy *Franklin Gothic Medium!*" Tessa squeaked. "It worked!"

"Watch your language, miss," I said absently. I snatched the paper up eagerly, and she ripped it right out of my hands.

"Simon! They are all here. Every knob has a label!"[79] When she stopped bouncing up and down,[80] I caught a view of the chart and found that it looked very much like the one Tessa had made. Indeed, everything was labeled.

79 Okay. Maybe my luck was changing. Was it a *lucky* day now? How many hours had actually passed? Tough to say, really.

80 Hard to do when you're glued to a sheet of glass, if you think about it.

The last row on the right (the E row, as we refer to it) had been smudged by some dark substance so that the writing was no longer legible, but the rest of it was clear. Tessa got out her own diagram, and we began to compare the two.

"He doesn't go into descriptions with his," she said, disappointed. "He just labels them."

"That's okay. Let's start with the ones that we have questions on. D2. That one made a sheep fall from the sky a couple times, but once it made that huge farting noise remember?"

"More than just the *noise*, if I recall correctly." Tessa said, giving me a significant look. "Look, he calls that one *Distraction*. That makes sense. It just does something to create a useful distraction."

"What about C5?" I said. "The dancing one."

"I've labeled that *Jig* on ours already. He calls it *Dance*."

"Cool. D3?"

"That one summons weird stuff, right? The broomstick, and the heffelone?

"The telephone, yeah."

"He calls that one *Random Item*."

"Pretty much sums up our experience with it. Not a very imaginative title, though," I noted. "Let's call it the *Summonator*."

"Whatever you say, Peanut."

I felt my cheeks flush again. Tessa said the *weirdest* things sometimes.

"Relax. It's a peanut joke. How about D4? He calls it

Inappropriate Affect."[81]

"That's the one that made me giggle," I said. "but let's not call it *Inappropriate Affect...*"

"How about *Giggle*?"

"Nice."

"D5 he calls *Sidestep*."

"That's the one that makes me disappear and then reappear a couple feet to the left," I said

"I like that. Let's keep that name. E1 he calls *Doppelgänger*. That's a little creepy, so I am going to label it *Clone*. We know what that one does... E2 he calls *Time Stop*. Pretty self-explanatory, and that seems to be your experience with it as well."

"Let's call that one *Pause*," I said.

"Whatever. He has that one circled in red with the word 'danger' written next to it."

"Yeah... It gets pretty weird when you start messing with the space-time continuum."

"Out of curiosity," she said, "did you notice that before or after you accidentally chopped me in half and nearly trapped me for all eternity in an alternate past?"

I cleared my throat awkwardly. "Before. What does he say about E3, *Daze*? That's the one that seems to knock the whole universe out for a second."

"He calls that one *The Anomaly*."

"I still think *Daze* is more succinct."

"Agreed. That's all but two from the left side that we

---

81 Inappropriate Affect is a psychological term that describes an unnatural emotional response.

have tested and labeled then. E4 and E5 he calls *Size* and *Thoughts*. I suppose we'll just have to go with his names for the rest of these."

"Should we try those two right now?" I said, eager for action. "I could just say 'Do the effects of turning the E4 knob,' and we could test it out right here!"

She gave me an expression like a mother would give to an impatient child. "Let's get them all just written *down* first, okay?" A6, he calls *Single Person Transport*. That's interesting. Isn't that the one that keeps summoning Ioden? A7 he calls…wait for it…"

"Oh no," I said.

She gave me an evil grin. A7 he calls *Epiphany*, which makes sense, given that's exactly what it does when you use it. So… I guess that settles that."

"Yeah, yeah," I said, waving her off. "What's next?"

"A8 through A10 he calls *Transportation*, *Do-Over*, and *Bouquet*."

"Whoa! Let me try *Transportation* really quick. Please?"

"Simmer down, Peanut," she snapped.

"Stop calling me that!"

"Stop acting like a legume,[82] then. On the *next* line, we

82 A legume is any member of the plant family more accurately known as Fabaceae or Leguminosae. There are 19,000 varieties of legumes, and legume plants (which can be trees, shrubs, or smaller things) always have a flower and stipulated leaves (whatever that means). I'm feeling uncharacteristically considerate right now, so I won't list all 19,000 varieties in this footnote, but some common legumes are: lentils, soybeans, peas, alfalfa, chickpeas, green beans,

have what he calls *Strength*, *For Diving*, *Enemy*, *Luck*, and *Sight*. That's B6 through B10."

"Hey! *For Diving*! We're underwater! Let's try that now and—"

"No! If you start trying out knobs now, who knows what will happen. We need to write these down and think things through before you do something crazy, and we never have a chance to again. Now sit there and eat your Hot Tamales."

"What's left of them," I grumbled, peaking into the nearly empty box.

"C6 through C10 read *Juvenile*, *Gravity*, *Unfathomable*, *Mass*, and *Inflation*. Are you getting all of these down?"

I assured her that I was, but we had to take a break so that she could check my work anyway.[83] Once she verified that I wasn't ruining her precious chart, she continued.

"D6 through D10 say *Lightning*, *Disarm*, *Lie*, *Slick*, and *The Strangeness*. Before you ask, I forbid you to try *The Strangeness* right now. This coat is strange enough, and if Rellik thought this knob was strange in comparison to all the other ones, I'd rather not be standing right next to you when you test it."

"Fair enough. What do you suggest we try first, then? Should we just go in order?"

"I think the first thing you should do is memorize all of these, just in case."

---

lima beans, silly beans, bumble beans, liver beans, spleen beans, gallbladder beans, pancreas beans, large intestine beans, stomach beans, and kidney beans.

83 Not that Tessa is a control freak or anything...

"Right." It *was* a good idea, so I did as she said. I was really careful, and took my time, so it took about one minute. When I was done, we decided to test B7 (*For Diving*) first, seeing as how we were underwater and everything. I said, "Do the effect of turning the knob B7, labeled *For Diving*. Peanuts."

"It's pea*nut*, Simon."

"Oh. Peanut."

Instantly, my hands and feet became large and floppy, and my fingers and toes connected to each other with a fleshy webbing. Slits opened up on the sides of my neck. Also, I suddenly could not breathe. Rather, I could inhale and exhale, sucking air in and out, but it didn't seem to help me at all, and I went on suffocating.

Tessa, who had either noticed that I was turning purple or saw the gills on my neck and put two and two together, shouted, "Turn E8, dummy! There's plenty of water right outside!"

I clutched at my throat. My air was gone. My mouth had changed anyway, and I didn't think I could have spoken even if I had air to do it with.

"Oh no," Tessa said, realizing my problem. "You can't speak. Use your mind, Simon. Use your mind! Do it in your head!"

What was she talking about? My head was swimming. I was starting to see stars.

Tessa lurched forward and slapped me hard in the face, falling on her own face in the process. "SAY IT IN YOUR HEAD!"

Turn E8, I thought frantically. *Turn E8. Turn E8! Turn E8!*

"PEANUT!" Tessa shouted.

Turn E8. Peanut! I thought.

Instantly I was floating in dark water. I was wearing the turncoat again. I could breathe! I gasped, sucking water into my lungs through my neck gills[84] and felt entirely strange. I had done it! I had used my mind to control the turncoat. That seemed almost, dare I say, *magical.* I pumped my fist through the water in triumph.

Something scratched at my arm, and I turned to see the bindle cage floating in the water beside me. Tessa's tiny form floundered inside it, clutching at her throat.

Comic Sans! When I'd turned E8, the coat had emptied *everything* from the pocket! I turned it again, and we were back inside. Tessa spluttered, gasping for air. Meanwhile, I began to suffocate again.

This was ridiculous. Why didn't I have more control over my magic? I focused my intention as hard as I could, thinking of Tessa staying inside, of me going outside, then turned E8 again with my mind. I really hoped it would work.

Tessa would be *really* mad if it didn't work…

It did. I was outside, breathing water through my gills again, and I was alone. I felt a little tingle in the pit of my stomach and couldn't help patting myself on the back for getting something right for once.

I started to swim and found that my webbed hands

---

84 Don't try this at home.

and feet lent themselves well to the process—I had never swum this fast before. I swam until I realized that I had no idea what direction I was going in. What if I was swimming straight down? I then remembered something I saw in a movie once: If scuba divers get disoriented underwater and don't know which way is up, they're supposed to blow out a bubble. The bubble will rise to the surface, instantly reorienting them.

I tried to blow out a bubble only to realize that since I had been breathing water this whole time, I had no air in my lungs and therefore no bubble-blowing powers. I turned B7 again and became my normal self. Then I turned E8 (*Stash*) and reappeared inside the turncoat Fluff grove.

"Well," Tessa said, wringing out her sweater sleeves and shivering. "That was fun."

"I totally used my mind to control the turncoat!" I said. "Like four times!"

Tessa grinned. "Pretty cool."

"*And* I can totally breathe underwater. Hold on just a second. I want to try something." I took a deep breath, turned E8 (with my mind again. It seemed easy now. Why had I never tried it before?), reappeared outside in the water, and blew a big bubble. It hung there for a second in front of my face.

Then it did nothing at all.

It just sat there.

I turned E8 again.

"Welcome back."

"Tessa," I said, "I don't know how to say this… I don't think there is an *up* out there."

She looked taken aback. "Well, that's freaky."

"Yeah. Also, that water tastes weird."

"Simon, if you're quite finished messing around, would you dry me off, please?"

"Oh, sorry." I did.

"What do you mean, the water tastes weird?" she said.

I licked my lips. It was a familiar taste. It reminded me of being sick, for some reason. "Chamomile. That water tastes like chamomile! Why would that be?"

Tessa shrugged. "Maybe you swallowed a bit too much, if you catch my drift."

"Maybe. Anyway, since we don't know what else to do, we might as well try a few more knobs, yeah?"

"Yeah… Hey, Simon, what do you suppose would happen if say, a giant orange shark ate the turncoat?"

"That's an oddly specific question," I said, following her gaze to the sky window above us. Sure enough, a giant orange shark seemed to be sniffing the turncoat.

"Can sharks even sniff?" Tessa said.

"Technically, no."[85]

The shark opened its huge, much-larger-than-your-standard-leather-jacket-sized mouth and swallowed the turncoat.

---

85 Sometimes, in high-stress or otherwise odd situations, you may find your mind begins to go numb, and you say silly things. It just so happens that having a giant orange shark sniff your magical turncoat is one of those situations.

18

KNAVE[86]

A knave; a rascal; an eater of broken meats; a base, proud, shallow, beggarly, three-suited, hundred-pound, filthy, worsted-stocking knave; a lily-livered, action-taking knave, a (kumquat); a glass-gazing, super-serviceable finical rogue; one-trunk-inheriting slave; one that wouldst be a bawd, in way of good service, and art nothing but the composition of a knave, beggar, coward, pandar, and the son and heir of a mongrel (kumquat): one whom I will beat into clamorous whining, if thou deniest the least syllable of thy addition.

—William Shakespeare[87]

"Ugh," Drake gasped, doubling over.

"Sorry," Loni said kindly, bending over and placing

86 A tricky, deceitful, or dishonest person.

87 Shakespeare's plays contain some of the highest high points and lowest low points of the English language. This is an example of the latter (It's from *King Lear*, if you were wondering). I include it here because, as you will see later, Drake really *needed* something nasty like this to say but didn't have anything at his disposal. I therefore offer this to you in case you ever find yourself in such a situation. It should be noted that I replaced the original naughty words in this quote with the word *kumquat*, which sounds very bad, but is actually just a tiny Asian fruit. Kumquats are a citrus fruit that look almost exactly like oranges, except that they are the size of olives. Unlike most other citrus fruits, the meat is sour, while the peel is sweet.

her hand flat on Drake's belly. Her palm glowed, and the wound knit together. "I didn't want our first night out to go like this," she whispered in his ear. "You've been so nice to me since you came to live with us. I've never met anyone like you before." She helped him stand up, then kissed him on the cheek, blushing slightly.

Drake nearly passed out at this, but whether from the kiss or the stab wound in his gut, we will not speculate. She helped him sit down, after which he sort of stared off into space with a pleasantly blank expression, still feeling the kiss on his cheek, no doubt, and feeling happily adrift in the cosmos.[88]

"Holy Helvetica," Tav said. "Can we get a move on?"

"It's not healed all the way," Loni told Drake. "I've only closed it. I need access to a special healing room to finish it, and the closest ones are in the castle. See? Now we have a legitimate reason to cross the lake. Not to mention that you don't pose nearly as much of a threat in your current condition."

"Is it safe?" Drake groaned, wincing. "It hurts."

"I've healed wounds like this for soldiers before. It's safe. Provided we get you to the castle in the next twenty minutes. After that, of course, you'll, you know..."

"Succumb to an agonizing death?" Tav suggested.

---

88 This phrase represents blatant thievery, as I lifted it straight out of a book by Kurt Vonnegut. He writes strange and thoughtful stories full of things that no one should ever say out loud. His books are worth a read, but not until you are older. We wouldn't want to cause the premature demise of any blissfully ignorant residents still lounging in the undisturbed palace of a young mind, would we? Or maybe we would. So it goes...

"Basically," she said.

"Okay, let's go," Drake said, pushing himself to his feet.

"Not so fast," Tav said. "That gives *him* a legitimate reason to go, but not me. Here, Drake. Your turn. Stab me." He handed Drake the knife.

"No," Drake said. "Here, you do it, Loni."

"I'm not stabbing anyone," Loni said. "This is *your* silly crusade. I'm just trying to help you out."

"Well, *I* can't stab anyone," Drake insisted.

"Come on, Drake, give me stab," Tav said. "You know you want to."

"I certainly do *not*!" Drake protested. "I, unlike you, am a decent person."

"A decent *minotaur,* maybe." Tav sniffed. "Though I doubt it. Minotaurs are supposed to be fierce, aren't they? You're about the farthest thing from fierce I've ever seen. I bet they make fun of you, don't they? The other freaks like your *people*? You don't even look the part." He laughed. "You can lick that green gob of goo as much as you like. I bet you *never* grow up." He rounded on Loni. "And *you*. You must be the most beautiful girl in Tarinea. Odd, sure, with the white hair and all, but beautiful. I'll say." He whistled. "And here you are liking *him*? What is *wrong* with you?" He shook his head. "What a waste."

Drake, teeth bared and eyes wide as pie pans, lurched forward and stabbed Tav in the gut.

"Ha!" Tav groaned, doubling over. "I knew you had it in you. Just needed a little push."

Drake was panting hard, nostrils flared.

"You shouldn't let him bait you like that, Drake," Loni said, but her voice shook slightly.

"So easy," Tav said. "People are *so* easily manipulated."

"Quiet you," Loni said. "You're a bully. I've half a mind to let you bleed."

But she didn't, of course. She raised her arm into the air, and one of the long black boats glided toward them. As it came, she placed her hand over Tav's stomach and closed the wound.

"Come on," she said, helping Drake into the boat. "Don't worry. They don't tip."

Tav boarded after them, and the boat began to move swiftly toward the castle.

Drake stared up at the giant blue castle that loomed over them and withdrew the now familiar ball of slime, the kulrakalakia, out of his pocket. He gave it a lick for luck and then dropped it in his boot for safekeeping.

"So," Drake said, giving Tav a hard look, "you didn't mean the things you said back there? You were just trying to make me stab you?"

Tav grinned. "I suppose we'll never know."

"I don't like you very much," Drake said.

"I know, Drake," Tav said. "I don't blame you. Simon's a good friend, I'm sure. He seems like a nice person."

"He is."

"I'm not, you know. Simon knows I'm not."

"Then why does he trust you?" Drake said.

Tav shrugged. "How should I know? Nice people tend to be far too trusting..."

Drake glowered, holding the wound in his gut. It was starting to feel firm. That couldn't be good.

"You're both sweating," Loni said. "Try not to talk so much. We're almost there."

She was proved right. A minute later their boat drew up alongside a low pier, and she hopped out, helping them follow. She led them to the castle doors, which stood twenty feet high, and knocked.

The sound was so soft against the huge doors that Drake was sure no one would hear, but a little window slid open almost instantly, revealing a flash of gold.

"Lolialoniakalli," Loni said, announcing herself. "Apprentice to the king's healer, Lolialokianalli. These two are wounded. I require the use of the healing halls."

The masked figure behind the door seemed to be looking something up.

"Your name is indeed listed, but it says here you only have clearance for entry during daytime hours. I cannot make exceptions."

"Sure you can." Tav grunted. He steadied himself, pulling up straight so he could look the guard in the eye.

The guard's mask tilted, the guard behind it no doubt taking in Tav's disheveled state.

"I cannot," he insisted. "I'm sorry. The rules are clear."

Tav groaned so believably that even Drake didn't know if he was faking or actually in that much pain. "Whoever wrote those rules isn't here, friend. You can do whatever you want. But if you *don't* let us in, I hope you'll have time to attend my funeral and tell my mother why your little rule book was more important than my life." He coughed, and blood spurted from his lips, spraying the ground. For an instant, Drake thought he saw something flash behind Tav's eyes. A light, perhaps. A little glint of power.

"Very well," the man said. "You may enter. But tell no one."

The doors swung open, revealing a high-ceilinged room with marble floors. Three members of the King's Guard stood in the entrance hall, red robed and bearing spears. They wore golden masks like the ones I had seen before (a cat, a horse, an elk, and a goat, in this case).

"Go with your wounded," said the guard who had opened the door. He wore the cat mask. "Return with them as soon as your work is finished."

"I will," Loni said. She hurried through a side door and up a set of spiraling stone steps. The walls and floor glowed blue, just like the exterior of the building, lighting their way.

"That was fast talking back there, Tav," Drake said as they began to climb. "I didn't think they were going to let us in."

"What can I say?" Tav said. "I have a sweet tongue."

"You have a gift for magical manipulation, more likely," Loni said. "I *saw* you use power back there. You hid it well, but I saw you. You better not ever try anything like that on me."

"Wouldn't think of it," Tav said, grinning.

"You mean you *made* him let us in with magic?" Drake said. He whistled. "I've never seen anything like that."

Tav chuckled. "It's what I do best."

They came to a landing, and she pushed them down a hallway that led to two rooms with wide doorways. The one on the left was apparently a guardroom of some sort.

"This way," she said, steering them into the other room. It was a round chamber with a floor of loose sand. It reminded Drake strongly of Grandma Loki's kitchen, except that there was a circular white stone in the middle of this room instead of a firepit, along with a countertop that ran around the entire outside wall, covered in potions, spices, instruments, and books.

Loni left them and went to work at the counter. A minute later she came back with two stone bowls. "Drink this," she said, handing Drake one of the bowls. "Half each."

He drank half the potion and handed it to Tav. "Ugh," he said. "Tastes like…like…"

"Raktorian goose feet boiled in an infusion of stillwater and yak bladder extract?" Loni suggested. "Because that's what it is. It's a pain limiter. It ensures that the pain won't kill you."

"Lovely," Tav said, shivering as he gulped it down.

"Pain?" Drake said. "It's not *that* bad."

Loni had picked up a long, roundish tool—like a mallet with a wide, flat head—and was placing the flat end onto the white stone in the center of the room. A second later it burst into flame. She brought the tool back, carrying the white flames on the end of it. It danced in the breeze as she walked.

"It's about to be." She thrust the end of her instrument at their bellies, striking them hard. First Tav, then Drake. Drake doubled over, screaming as the white fire swirled around his middle and vanished into his gut. It felt as if he was on fire. It was the most intense pain he'd ever known. He was going to die! He…

"Hey," Drake said slowly, "I feel better."

"Me too," Tav said, inspecting his belly. "No burn marks, either. You know, I think that was the most painful thing I've ever experienced."

"Me too," Drake said. "Wasn't there another way?"

"Sure," Loni said. "Lots. But they take time. This is the quickest. Now it's done."

"Right," Tav said. "I think I saw a guardroom across the hall. Let's go put on some of those robes. Easier to move around if we look like King's Guards, don't you think? They might even let us into the armory."

The guardroom was packed with supplies. A cell with iron bars ran along one wall, while another was covered with chairs where people could sit and change. The third wall held racks of swords, spears, and the red robes of the King's Guard. Atop a high shelf sat rows and rows of golden animal masks.

"No weapons," Drake said. "There's been enough stabbing today."

"Sure," Tav said. "Hey, Drake, look at this. How do you think this works?"

"What do you mean?" Drake said, stepping in front of the open cell door beside Tav. "I guess they use it to lock people up. What's so—"

Tav shoved Drake hard in the back, then kicked him so that he fell forward through the cell door.

Drake leaped to his feet, but the bars clanged shut behind him.

"What are you doing?" Loni said, grabbing Tav's arm.

Tav whipped one of the short swords off the rack and pressed it to Loni's neck. "Hush, Loni. We wouldn't want to start a commotion."

"Don't do this," Drake pleaded. "Please."

"I *am* doing this, Drake," Tav said, pushing Loni into a chair.

"I don't understand," Drake said. "Why?"

"Because I don't trust you, Drake. Or rather, I *do* trust you. I trust you to be yourself—a good person—and I can't risk having a good person with me tonight. I've got to get that spear, and I can't risk you spoiling it."

"But I could help you," Drake said. He shook the door, but it didn't budge. He couldn't get stuck in here.

"Oh?" Tav said. He rummaged through the rack of red cloaks and put one on. "And what if it proves difficult to steal the spear? What if they catch us? What if I have to kill someone? Are you going to help me kill someone, Drake?"

Drake gulped.

"I didn't think so. You're dead weight, minotaur."

Drake raised his hand and pointed at the lock. He

wasn't the best Bright in the world, but he could move objects fairly well with his mind. Maybe he could shift the tumblers of the lock enough to… But no. It wasn't working.

"Your magic won't work in there," Tav said. "It was built to hold *wizards*."

"Why are you like this?" Drake said, leaning against the bars. "How can you be so cruel?"

"Well," he said slowly, "for one thing, I'm not quite as young as I let on."

As he spoke, the lines of his jaw sharpened, his eyes sank deeper into his face, and he grew taller. Much taller. "Broca was looking for a child, after all, and I needed a master. *He* saw through my façade, I don't doubt. Hard to fool a wizard like him up close. No doubt he's curious to see what I make of his challenge, regardless of my age. You and Simon didn't see through my little disguise, though, I take it?"

Drake shook his head, appalled at this new revelation. Tav was easily sixteen. Seventeen, maybe.

"As for the rest of it, *why* I am the way I am, it's a sad story, Drake." Tav walked along the shelf of masks now, touching each one in turn. "The story of an ambitious boy who was always second best. A brother who was always better. A father who was an idiot. A grandfather who was always too busy.[89] They never listened to me, you know.

89 Tav sure sounds like he had a lonely childhood, doesn't he? Strange that in a world where people can connect instantly from opposite sides of the planet, so many can be so lonely? Life is convenient in the twenty-first century. Easy, when it comes to boiling water, making

They never even *listened* to my ideas. They aren't the only geniuses in the family. They'll see. They should have listened. They'll listen now. Broca will teach me what I need to know, and then I'll become…what I am meant to be. They'll never see it coming. They never saw me to begin with."

Something twisted in Drake's gut at Tav's words. It felt like the wound opening up again, but deeper. A sense of foreboding. "Tav?" Drake said slowly.

"Ah," Tav said, reaching for a mask on the back of the shelf. "Yes. I was wondering, and here it is, just as you said. I suppose this is where it begins."

He held up the mask for Drake's inspection, grinning as he did so. Drake's breath caught in his chest. It was a mask he'd seen before. In paintings. In countless books. In the darkness of the tomb of Rone.

The Jackal's mask.

---

dinner, or traveling a hundred miles. No longer are such tasks the sole occupation of an hour, a day, a week. No longer is dinner appreciated because it took all day to make, nor must a family band together to make that meal happen day in and day out. No longer are our days spent in monotony, working side by side, striving hard not to freeze to death, and gazing at the stars, *conversing* by candlelight when the sun sets. We have microwaves and desk jobs and a truly endless entertainment stream to keep us company in our separate rooms at night. But, of course, a life lived thus is inherently counterfeit. Life is still about survival, the survival of the human soul, the human psyche, the human family, and no one survives alone. So remember, kids, when you're done reading or watching today, turn off the TV, put *down* this book, leave your room, speak to another human, get into trouble, talk to your mother, visit a shut-in, walk your dog, learn to play chess, tickle a baby, go on an adventure, and take someone with you. In short, live.

"No," Drake whispered.

Tav laughed, placing the mask on his head.

Loni leaped forward, raising her hands. Something sparkled at the tips of her fingers, but Tav kicked backward viciously, striking her in the gut and throwing her to the ground.

"You—" Drake stuttered. "You… You… YOU!"

Tav threw back his head and laughed, the Jackal's face gleaming. "Imagine my surprise when you and Simon started telling me about *myself*, my grandfather, my brother. Rok. Rellik. The most famous wizards in your history. I guess my full name, Tavronan, is forgotten eventually, or you would have recognized me on the spot. Lucky that. I've always gone by Tav, but Rone works just as well. Has a nice ring to it, actually."

Rone lifted Loni off the floor and tied her hands behind her back with a length of rope from the shelves.

"Are you going to kill Simon?" Drake said.

Rone paused, then cinched the rope tight and began backing out of the room, Loni in tow. "I haven't decided. Tricky business, messing with the future. Dangerous. And he's my mortal enemy, it seems. Killing him before he's born?" He shook his head. "I don't know. I left you alive, and look at how much you've helped me already."

He paused in the doorway, placing Loni in front of him like a prisoner. "Take me to the armory, girl," he said. "No tricks, or you'll never kiss poor Drake here again."

"Don't hurt her!" Drake said.

"Don't worry yourself," Tav said. "I'm not as bad as I

seem." He paused. "You know, for a smart guy you didn't pick the best girl to get a crush on, Drake. You're the one that told me Tarinea is going to be destroyed, and we're all going to die. How did you think your little love story would end?"

Drake didn't know what to say to that, but he shoved the problem out of his mind. "Are you going to kill Simon? Tell me!"

The Jackal's mask glinted in the light from the hallway. "I guess we'll just have to wait and see."

Then they were gone.

1. Incapable of being fully explored or understood.
2. (of water or a natural feature) Impossible to measure the extent of

—Google[90]

Don't believe what anyone says about what happens next. I'll tell you the *real* story:

While Tessa was shouting, "Eek! Eek! A shark! A shark! Save me, Simon!" and giant shark teeth were ripping into the sides of the coatroom all around us, I remained completely calm. I rolled up my sleeves, set my jaw, turned A3 (*Curse*), and then E8 (*Stash*). Both with my mind, of course.

Then I *broke* the shark.[91]

Everything my body touched—mouth, teeth, shark face—blew into about a puzillion[92] pieces.

My work done, I turned E8 again and reentered the coatroom.

90 A magical internet genie whose lamp gets rubbed 3.5 billion times per day.

91 If you've never broken a shark before, I don't recommend it. Sharks, as it turns out, have all kinds of little parts to them. If you *do* have to break a shark, try not to do it while you are *inside* the shark.

92 An unquantifiable number somewhere between 12 and 98,000,000,000,000,000,001.

"Nice work, Simon. Ugh! Is that shark guts all over you? Simon Fayter, get your peanut-brittle buns back outside right now and wash off."

"Sure," I said.

Then (with rather poor timing) a bright-pink child's bicycle appeared beneath me. Complete with training wheels, handlebar basket, and honky horn.

"Simon," Tessa said slowly, "did you just test out another knob?"

"Maybe," I said evasively. "It's possible that, you know…"

"What? That a bike just fell out of your *pants*?"

"Okay… So I tested another knob. A8 (*Transportation*)." I honked the honky horn.

"I *guess* that's a form of transportation… Um… Turn it again?"

I mentally commanded the knob to turn again, and nothing happened. Apparently this was one of the knobs that only worked once a day. Also, apparently that rule applied even while I was inside the turncoat. Go figure.

I went back outside and washed off after that, since Tessa wouldn't say another word to me until I did. As I was doing so, staring around at the unfathomable expanse of dark water in which I floated, I pondered our predicament. By the time I went back inside, I had made up my mind.

"It's unfathomable, Tessa," I said.

"What?"

"This situation. This big sea that we are in, with no up

and down. No surface to find. It's *unfathomable*."

Tessa's eyes widened. "No, Simon. No, don't you turn that one ye—"

It was too late, of course. I had already mentally turned C8 (*Unfathomable*). I couldn't help myself. It was too perfect!

A strange thing happened then. A thing which, I admit, I do not understand to this day.

A man appeared in our little clearing. It was a kindly faced, middle-aged man. He had a black bowler hat and carried a polished black cane with a silver ram's-head handle.

"Oh!" he said, looking around. "Oh my. Well… greetings!"

"Uh," I said. "Who are you?"

"An excellent question," he said approvingly. "And, in my experience, the very best place to start. My name is Archibald." He tipped his hat to Tessa. "And who, if I may be so bold, might *you* be?"

We didn't say anything.

"Ah, yes." He nodded. "Wise to withhold your names from a stranger who has appeared so mysteriously. Let me assure you, however, that I mean you no harm. Did you summon me here?"

"*He* did," Tessa said, pointing at me.

"I see. Usually goes the other way around for me, you know," he said with a chuckle. He checked the silver watch that hung from a chain on his vest and gave a low whistle. The hands, I saw, were spinning wildly, as if desperately searching for the time but unable to find it.

"Time might be a bit different here," I offered. "Or we might have accidentally pulled you into a different time altogether. Sorry…" He seemed like a very nice person.

Archibald straightened one of the white gloves that he wore. "I beg your pardon, but where *is* here?"

"Sector 99," Tessa said. "Of Tarinea."

He didn't look like that meant anything to him. "Do you know where that is in relation to Caraway?" he asked.

"Never heard of it. But Tarinea is in the third seal, if I remember right."

"Hmmm," Archibald said, gazing around at the strange little clearing. "If I didn't know any better, I would say that I had wandered right out of my story and into another. Do you know why I am here?"

"Nope."

He scratched his head. "Well, generally I help people with things. Serve people, you could say. Is there any way in which I could serve you, do you suppose? What do you need? What's going on here?"

"Well," I said, wondering where to begin.

"We're stuck inside a magical coat," Tessa said, "because we went into a weird place looking for a powerful wizard and found it filled from top to bottom with black water."

"Fascinating," Archibald said, eyes twinkling. "You must want to talk to this wizard very badly. I suppose the fate of the world rests upon it, and all that?"

"Naturally," I said.

Archibald beamed. "Well, then, if you are unable to get to him—and it certainly sounds like you are, have you considered summoning him to you?"

"Uh," I said, "I don't know how I would try that."

"Well," Archibald said, "that may be why I am here."

"Huh?" Tessa said, perking up. "You know Xerith?"

Archibald shook his head. "No, no, I'm afraid not. But I *do* possess a most powerful summoning tool." When he said this, he withdrew a small silver bell from his vest pocket. "It is designed to summon the person I always need most. So, if I am truly in a different universe, and I have been brought here to aid you, it follows that it might now summon the person *you* need most." He looked absolutely pleased with himself at this declaration. Then he frowned slightly. "Of course, I may be wrong. Strictly speaking, it is built to summon one specific person from my world, but I'm afraid it's my best idea at present."

"What if it doesn't work?" I said.

He shrugged. "Then nothing will happen." He cleared his throat. "Alternatively, a young lady friend of mine might suddenly join us in our confusion. Who can say for sure?"

"Only one way to find out," I said, grinning. I liked this guy.

He lifted his cane in a salute. "Precisely. Would you like to do the honors?" He handed the delicate silver bell to me and waved in encouragement. "Go on. Ring it."

I did.

Nothing happened.

It didn't even make any noise.

Archibald was still waving his hand, so I rang the bell again.

There was a cacophonous boom, a flash of blue light, and an explosion of smoke, as if lightning had struck the ground directly in front of me. When the smoke cleared, the Tike stood before me, looking more than a little dazed.

"Holy Minion Pro!" I exclaimed, rushing to the Tike and scooping her up in a hug.

"Ha!" Archibald said. "That's exactly what it does for me—though admittedly with less melodrama! I don't suppose this is the one woman in the world that you care for above any other, and that you are bonded to her by oath, love, and fate?"

"Pretty much," Tessa grumbled.

"SIMON FAYTER!" the Tike shouted, pushing me away. "WHAT IN THE NAME OF RELLIK'S SOUR TOE JAM HAVE YOU DONE?"

"All right, then," Archibald said brightly, scooping the little bell out of my hands with deft precision. "I think I should be going now. If you don't mind, young sir, doing, you know, whatever it is you did to bring me here, and sending me on my way?"

I grinned, turned C8, and Archibald vanished.[93]

"Well," Tessa said, popping the last strawberry in her

93 If this whole thing seems extremely random to you, that's because it is. My pseudo publishing counterpart/patsy/decoy/secret cover identity, Austin J. Bailey, tells me that Archibald is a character who features prominently in his other *fictional* work. Why the turncoat should summon him into reality—a different reality than he was ever

mouth and tossing the empty bowl across the clearing, "that was *really* weird, and pretty much useless."

"What is going on?" the Tike demanded.

I held out my arms to her again. "Welcome to the party!"

"What is going *on*?"

"I may have, sort of, you know, slipped into the distant past while trying to look for a way out of that hard decision I have to make in the tomb of Rone. I might have traveled back hundreds of years in time to the height of Tarinea and accidentally brought Drake and Tessa with me. And now you! I'm so glad you could make it."[94]

"Simon, what possessed you to do something so foolish and cowardly?" the Tike said, then she turned. "Tessa, *where are your legs*? Tessa? Tessa, are you all right?"

Tessa, who a moment earlier had been listening raptly to our little conversation, was now staring upward with intense focus. Her mouth dropped open in a silent scream, which was in fact, not silent for long.

"AYEYEYEYEYEYEYEYEYEEYE!"

I looked up and saw exactly what Tessa's scream described:

A giant eye, golden brown, filling my view from side to side. The water was gone outside the turncoat. The darkness was gone too. All that remained was the eye. It

---

made to exist in—is beyond me. Maybe that's why Rellik named this knob *Unfathomable*: because it did things that no rational person could ever possibly understand.

94 She almost wasn't in this book at all! Yikes…

was unfathomably[95] large, as if the endless ocean that held us was but a teardrop by comparison.

The eye blinked, and our universe exploded.

95 There's that word again. Watch out…

Rood: *Go away! Whatever I broke, I'm sorry!*
Master Tel: *You have broken the locks to Nun's books of wizardry!*
Rood: *I know the Great Shout is forbidden, but it's a thing of impulse rather than premeditation, and I was overwhelmed by impulse. Please shut up!*

—The Riddle-Master of Hed[96]

Drake punched the iron bars of his cell.

It had been twenty minutes since the others had left. What could have happened in that amount of time? Thus far his efforts to escape had been unsuccessful. He couldn't stop thinking about Loni. Had they made it to the armory? Had they stolen the spear? Was she safe? What would Tav—*Rone* do to her?

He closed his eyes, forcing himself to be calm. He reached out with his mind again and tried to invade the lock. Somehow, it was like it didn't even exist. Usually he could find things with his mind, feel them, step inside them. That's how it worked, being a Bright. It was all

96 By Patricia A. McKillip. This is from a scene in chapter two. Yes, it's one of my all-time favorite books. No, I didn't steal the concept of a mind shout from her. Where would you get an idea like that?

about your mind. Using it well inside your own head, and then pushing past the boundaries of your own skull to influence the external world. Except, inside this cell, it was as if there *was* no external world.

A prison for wizards, indeed.

He shook the cell door with all his puny strength, and it rattled slightly. Well, *that* was the biggest effect he'd had on it yet.

He took out his sling and aimed a stone at the lock. Imbuing it with all the destructive mojo he could muster, he released the stone. It didn't even hit the door! It just slowed suddenly, turned out of its path, and fell harmlessly to the floor.

Drake screwed up his face in rage. This wasn't fair. It was so frustrating! Why had fate sent him on a mission to save the world without giving him proper time to prepare? Why had he followed Tav into this room? Why had he been so *stupid*? How could he be so powerless?

He summoned all his frustration, all his anger at the situation, and channeled it into a silent, explosive shout. The brightscream, it was called. The most raw, unwieldy, destructive force a Bright could summon. It leveled buildings to the ground. It had, in the hands of Maxilus the Great, once split a mountain in half. It was illegal in seventeen star systems and grounds for expulsion from Skelligard, so it wasn't like he had tried it before.

Still, he'd read about it, and he thought he knew how it was done. He felt power, *pure* power, explode out of him, and for an instant it seemed as if he'd done it. But the force of his brightscream fell against the cell door with all the feeble potency of a toddler's sneeze. It had no effect whatsoever, except to raise a tiny puff of dust into the air near an iron crossbar.

Drake sank onto the small cot in the cell with a groan. What was the use? He couldn't escape. He had failed Loni, who was now at the mercy of a young man destined to become the most evil wizard in the history of the universe. He had failed Simon, his best friend, who had trusted him to see this mission through.

Poor Simon. He had no idea what was coming! What would Tav choose to do to him? Would he kill him? Would Drake and Tessa and the Tike and all the others just vanish suddenly, when Simon was gone? Erased from the past before he could be born in the future? Drake scratched and rubbed his head, trying to alleviate the aching in his mind, and discovered that his long minotaur hair was gone. He looked like himself again. He must have let his disguise fall away in his efforts with the brightscream. Not that it mattered now. If the guards found him, there was nothing they could do to him that would be worse than what he was going through already.

He glared at the door, trying not to think, trying to just *hate* it. But his mind didn't work like that. It never had. It whirred with thoughts and ideas, analyses and classifications on the bars.

Black. Strong. Unbending. Steel with a high iron content. Firm but not brittle. Imbued with ancient magic. Unresponsive to any magic he could throw at it.

Unresponsive to *anything* he did, except for physically shaking the door. Unresponsive to everything but direct physical force.

He cocked his head.

Direct physical force…

He stood up and kicked the door. It made a low, metallic ringing sound. He picked up the cot and smashed it against the bars, and they rang and wobbled slightly.

Direct physical force. That was it! The cage had been designed to hold wizards! It was impregnable to magical attack but not direct physical force. That was its only weakness.

He looked around the room with new excitement, searching for something he could use on the door. He broke a short wooden leg off the bottom of the cot and jammed it between the bars. It wasn't really long enough to create much leverage, but it was better than nothing. He pulled with all his might, trying to pry the bars open slightly, but the old wood cracked and broke under the strain, and he stumbled back. He threw the broken chunk of wood away in frustration and looked around for something else, but there was nothing else in the cell.

Just him.

He stared at his puny minotaur hands and felt a familiar anger bubble up inside.

How long? How long would he have to go on like this? How long would he not be what he was supposed to be? If he were as strong as he was supposed to be, as big as he was supposed to be—if he were like the others, his father, his brothers, ANY OTHER MINOTAUR OVER TWELVE YEARS OLD, would he still be in this situation? He'd seen Kodakus the Wild in a frenzy once. Kodakus was Drake's second cousin, once removed on his mother's side—not exactly the *biggest* minotaur in the world, but he had still ripped a boulder in half. If he were any other minotaur, would he be able to peel the door off this cell?

Any. Other. Minotaur.

Drake ripped off his boot and shook it so that the kulrakalakia tumbled out. He picked up the fist-sized ball of slime and growled at it. The kulrakalakia had failed him too. It had worked for his grandfather, when he had been late. But it hadn't worked for Drake. Oh, no. *Nothing* worked for Drake.

"Well, are you going to eat it?" a deep voice boomed.

Drake started, spinning around to find who had spoken, but no one was there. He recognized the words. They danced around in his head frequently. That's what *Simon* had said right after they'd made the kulrakalakia.

"Up here, you hairless bovine."

Drake looked up. "Leto?"

The tiny dragon was lounging on the flat edge of a crossbar near the ceiling.

"What are you doing here?"

Leto leveled his tiny sparkling eyes at Drake. "I said, are you going to eat that?"

The rabbit-hole went straight on like a tunnel for some way, and then dipped suddenly down, so suddenly that Alice had not a moment to think about stopping herself before she found herself falling down a very deep well.

—Lewis Carroll[97]

When I say *exploded*, I don't want you to get the wrong idea. It didn't hurt or anything. It was a *gentle* explosion. I suppose if you could have been standing in the little seaside cabin with the man whose eye we had seen earlier, you would have simply witnessed an old, grandfatherly figure lift one of a dozen teacups off his mantelpiece, set it on his little round kitchen table, and

97 From *Alice's Adventures in Wonderland*. The story continues: "Either the well was very deep, or she fell very slowly, for she had plenty of time as she went down to look about her and to wonder what was going to happen next. First, she tried to look down and make out what she was coming to, but it was too dark to see anything; then she looked at the sides of the well, and noticed that they were filled with cupboards and book-shelves; here and there she saw maps and pictures hung upon pegs. She took down a jar from one of the shelves as she passed; it was labelled 'ORANGE MARMALADE', but to her great disappointment it was empty: she did not like to drop the jar for fear of killing somebody, so managed to put it into one of the cupboards as she fell past it."

peer into it. After eyeing the contents of the teacup for a moment, he winked, and…

With a sound like a thunderclap, I landed on a yellow crocheted rug. A wave of chamomile tea splashed out with me, spraying a good portion of the comfortably furnished cabin that I had landed in.

"You broke my shark," a trembling voice said.

I hopped to my feet and found myself face to face with the oldest man I'd ever seen. I mean, *old* doesn't begin to describe his state. He was basically fossilized. His hair and beard were long and white and braided with gold. His nose hair was white too, and it hung down halfway past his top lip.[98] His skin was so thin that it was practically transparent, so that his face and hands were like faded street maps of crisscrossing arteries and veins. Something about his bearing told me he had once been tall, but he was now shorter than I was, his small body wrapped in a cloak of royal blue. One of his eyes was white, the other the cold steely blue of a winter sky.

"Pardon me," he said, passing a hand in front of his face. When he removed the hand, the long nose hairs fell away, now neatly trimmed. "It's been a few hundred years since I had a visitor.

"Xerith?"

The man laughed. "Sure. Sure. Have a seat, Simon."

He gestured to a curved bench with embroidered cushions that surrounded a little breakfast nook at one end of the cabin, and I sat down, resting my arms on the

98 Too much information?

table. He moved very slowly, and with much shuffling and creaking, to a low rocking chair a few feet away and eased himself into it. The room around me was small (I could easily have spit to the other side) but comfortable. There was a tiny sink and counter on the opposite end from where I sat, and a bed and a small wood-burning fireplace in the middle. Fire glowed inside it.

"Where are my manners?" the man said. "You're all wet." He waved a hand, and my clothes ruffled in a warm breeze. Afterward, they were instantly dry. "I didn't mean to spill you all over the floor, of course. Clumsy of me." His voice was raspy, as if rarely used. "Welcome to Brocéliande, Simon."

"Where?"

"Brocéliande." He opened his arms, motioning at our quaint surroundings. "It's my...*retirement* home."

I glanced around again and for the first time looked out the windows. There were four of them, one on each side. Through one, I saw a gray and lonely-looking forest glade, complete with a lake. Through another, a beautiful sandy beach with soft waves glinting under a purple sunset. The third looked out over rolling green hills, summer sunshine, and yellow trees shaped like lollipops. The last one looked out on an underwater scene—blue with light filtering down from above, glowing fish, and a gorgeous coral reef. I felt entirely unsure whether the cabin was in the woods somewhere or sitting at the bottom of the ocean.

"Uh...okay," I said. "Sorry to...barge in."

"No problem!" He chortled. "That's why I keep the cups, you know."

I glanced at the teacup on the table. It was white porcelain, with the word "Tarinea" emblazoned on the side in gold letters. I stood up and peered into it. I could see, very clearly, the little Fluff clearing inside the turncoat, as though I were looking through the domed roof. Tessa and the Tike stood there. Tessa was pointing at me, gesturing wildly.

"Whoa," I said.

Xerith chuckled. "Yes. My seacups, I call them. Both because they are filled with chamomile sea, and because they allow me to see into other worlds. Or more accurately, they allow wizards from other worlds to come and see *me*, if they need to." He yawned. "It rarely happens anymore. Do you know the last person who came to me for advice wore those exact same boots? He was your predecessor, I believe, though you are visiting me from a time *before* he did. Aren't you a little young to be traveling through time?"

"Yes, sir," I said. "Sorry, did you just say I'm visiting you *before* Rellik did?"

"Sure."

"But if he hasn't visited you yet, how do you remem—"

"Time is a little *different* on Brocéliande, Simon. I wouldn't worry about it. Make your hair go white." He winked at me.

"Right."

"Rellik wore that coat as well," he said, giving me a significant look.

I felt my sides and realized that I was wearing the turncoat again. But… how could I be wearing it if Tessa and the Tike were still *inside* it in the cup?

"Ah, yes," Xerith said. "Rellik had *questions* about the coat too. I told him the same thing I am going to tell you."

"Which is?" I said eagerly.

"That it is very rude to solve another wizard's mystery." He gave me a sly grin, and his eyes twinkled.

"Are you serious?" I said. I couldn't help it. I couldn't believe he was going to dodge my questions after I came all this way to see him!

"Sometimes," he said. "Though I am giving you a bit of a hard time. There is one question I can't answer, but I will tell you, as I told him, that you will have to overcome your need to use the coat as a channeling vessel."

"How do I do that?"

He touched his finger to his nose. "And *there* it is."

"The question you can't answer?"

"Precisely."

"Because it's better if I find the answer myself?"

He laughed. "Because I don't know. Magic isn't an exact science, you know. I *can* tell you that you're spilling all *sorts* of power out right here." He pointed to a spot near the top of the right panel of the turncoat.

"Really?" I said, not sure if I was supposed to feel embarrassed. "Sorry. I don't mean to…uh…*leak* or anything."

"No, no, no," he said, waving a hand. "I mean you are channeling most powerfully through the vessel in that region."

"Oh." I checked to see which knob was closest to the point he had indicated.

"B9," I said. "*Luck!* That makes total sense! That's how my power usually manifests! As luck!" I turned the knob and felt instantly unlucky. I turned it again.

Lucky.

I turned it again.

Unlucky.

I turned it again.

Lucky.

I turned it again and caught my foot on his crocheted rug, tripped, and fell face forward into Xerith's lap.

"Oof!" he grunted. "You better make sure you leave that one on the right setting!"

"Right. Sorry." I turned it again, just to be safe. "This is so *weird…*"

It was cool too, of course. I mean, I had found the end of my lucky and unlucky days. I was finally in control! And yet, there were so many things I still didn't understand.

"Oh, yes," Xerith said. "The mystery continues. The answers don't all come at once. Generally they come as quickly as we are ready for them, but far slower than we would like. Rellik, for instance, was quite powerful in his own right before the… What do you call it? The *breaking*. But afterward, when he became the only wizard in your universe who could touch all six branches of magic, he had quite a hard time. Said the magic had changed. He was like a schoolboy again. Very frustrated." Xerith shook his head, frowning at the memory. "Though he was excited to finally understand why his coat had all those little pockets in it." He smiled. "That had always troubled him."

"What?" I said.

"Well, you can imagine, when the coat was given to him as a boy, how confused he must have been at all the pockets. It wasn't until later that he understood their use. Not uncommon with channeling vessels, or predestinated wizard garb, for that matter. Why, my own cloak had a strange opening sewn into the left armpit whose use was a complete mystery to me as a boy, and I wouldn't learn the secret until three hundred years later, when I needed to make an emergency shelter using nothing but my cloak and the bones of a yugyug."

"What pockets?" I said.[99] "Do you mean these five here?" I opened the right side of the jacket, pointing out the pockets on the E row.

"Balding Baskerville!" Xerith exclaimed. "What's happened to all the little pockets? Why, you've only got five left!"

"What? No. I got it like this, I swear. It only ever *had* five pockets, the rest are just knobs."

"Nonsense," Xerith said, slapping the arm of the rocking chair. "It had *fifty* pockets. One for each knob. One for each piece of the broken bloodstone."

---

99 It goes to show you how excited I was that I didn't even think to ask what a yugyug was.

I stared at him, dumbfounded. "Each piece," I mumbled, trying to grasp at the meaning of it. I opened the E6 (*Travel*) pocket and took out the bloodstone.

"Each pocket?" I said. "This one has always been in here, I just didn't…" Suddenly, it was all making sense. Fifty bloodstones. Fifty knobs. Fifty pockets.

"You have to put all of the bloodstones back in the pockets!" I exclaimed, smacking myself in the head. It was so simple.

"Obviously."

"I mean, for it to work properly! The bloodstone, that is. It was one piece, right? But then Rok broke it and scattered it."

"Right."

"So if I want to use it again, I have to put it back together. But I *can't* just put it back together, because it's an incredibly magical object made by the Zohar, or because it was broken by its own power, so it can only be healed by its own power, or something."

"Yes. Or something."

"So you put them all in their pockets, turn the knobs and, and… And then what?"

He raised his eyebrows. "And then what *indeed*."

"You don't know?"

"How should I? I've never done it!"

"But Rellik did. Didn't he?"

"*Did* he?" Xerith asked.

"You mean you weren't watching?"

Xerith shrugged. "I don't see everything you know. I'm not God."

I looked around the little cabin, looking out the windows into his various worlds, considering what he had told me. "You're sure?"

"Quite sure. Met him once. Nice man. A little odd…"

"No, I mean you're sure you don't know what happened to Rellik when he reunited the bloodstones?"

Xerith laced his fingers together thoughtfully, then went on as if he hadn't heard me. "I *am* something more than a wizard these days, I'll grant you that. Maybe a consulting demigod or an angel. That would be more accurate. An angel, going to and fro[100] in this world and that, poking, prodding, shaping. The truth is, I'm what you'll be someday. There are three of us, you know, the *great* wizards. The ones destined to travel out of our universes and into others, reshaping the past, changing the future. I was the first. You are the second."

"And the third?" I said.

"Weeks?" Xerith looked startled. "Good heavens, stay away from *him*. If you meet him, run the other way. Man's a complete mess."

"What about Rellik? I'm his heir, right? Why isn't he

---

100 For every high there is a low/for every to there is a fro/To and fro/Stop and go/That's what makes the world go round./You must set your sights upon the heights/don't be a mediocrity/Don't just wait and trust to fate/And say, that's how it's meant to be/It's up to you how far you go/If you don't try you'll never know/And so my lad as I've explained/Nothing ventured, nothing gained. —From *The Sword in the Stone.*

one of your three? He's the most powerful wizard who ever lived!"

Xerith gave me a kind smile. "He was the most powerful to have lived in *your* universe, perhaps. Until you. I am talking about wizards whose power and influence transcend their own universes. Growing beyond the boundaries in which they were born, possessed of powers too grand for a mortal to hold, we range across the whole of creation, seeking to bless the entire living races…"

He waved his hand. "Or something like that. I, for example, have lived in several universes, playing several roles, for several thousand years, wearing numerous faces and names, as you will. Tholoth, they call me in the Stenzajan universe. Rustes in Hamlastathari. Jobeth in Brodeulia. And two dozen others. In your universe, I am known by two names. Xerith, as you have come to know me, and Merlin.

"*What*?" I said. "Merlin? Like in *The Sword in the Stone*?"

Xerith waved a hand dismissively. "That film wasn't exactly biographical."

I sat back in my seat and felt myself go slightly cross-eyed.

"Odd sensation, isn't it? Your head exploding? Let me make you some tea." He swirled his finger in the air, and a teacup zoomed out of a cupboard and landed on the table. The teapot flew over from the stove and filled the cup while a bowl hopped out of the windowsill and began dishing spoonfuls of sugar into my cup. "Say when."

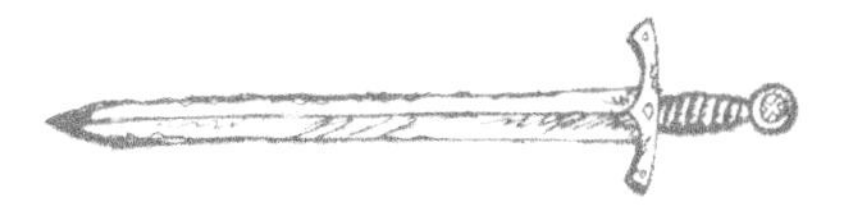

"There's one thing I don't get," I said after several swallows of tea had settled my mind a bit.

"More than *one* thing, actually, but go on."

"Rellik. Why—"

"Rellik did not become what he was meant to," Merlin said sadly. "I don't know why. I suspect he stepped up to the edge of the brink and did not dare to jump."

"What brink?" I said.

"The brink of power. The power to fix what was broken in your world. The power to heal your people."

"Someone told me," I said slowly, "that he was unwilling to pay the price."

"Ah, yes. The price. It is a heavy thing. Hard to pay. Difficult for everyone. He didn't pay it, so you were sent to become what he could not."

"But what's the price?" I said. "What will happen if I unite the bloodstones?"

"You will have power, I imagine. And you will see the way to heal your universe. And you will see the cost. And then..." He took a long, deep breath. "Then you will choose."

"But what's the price?"

He shrugged. "Different for everyone. And the same. The price of all power is essentially the same. Change. And loss. And often pain. Death too. Death of an old self, old ideas, old dreams. To walk the razor's edge and never faint. To climb to heights unbreathable and still breathe. The kind of power we are talking about requires *total* sacrifice. You will give up *everything* you love. Nothing less will suffice."

I stared at him blankly. "I don't understand."

He sighed. "I know. But now at least you can't say I didn't warn you. I wouldn't worry, Simon. It's not something you need to understand in advance."

I finished my tea in silence, lost in thought. When I looked up, Xerith—*Merlin*, whoever he was—was snoring softly in his rocking chair.

I cleared my throat, and he snorted awake. "Ah, sorry. I suppose you'll want to be going now. Hope you liked the tea. Come back, you know, when you've done something interesting. Just put your finger in the seacup. That will take you back."

"But..." I objected. "I haven't even asked you what I came to ask you! How do I defeat the draculadon? What am I going to do about my friends in the tomb? Is there any way out?"

Xerith shook his head. "*Don't* defeat the draculadon. Why would you want to kill such a creature? You are bonded with a dragon, are you not? Listen to what he tells you. You don't need my help with that. As to the second matter, no. There is no way out. You're going to have to choose."

"But—"

"It's a no-win situation," Xerith said. "All great leaders eventually—"

"I know, I know. I've been thinking about it. It's like

the *Kobayashi Maru*, right? But Captain Kirk found a way around that. I need *you* to help me find a way around *this*."

Xerith stared at me blankly.[101] "I'm not sure what you're going on about, Simon, but there *is* no way out of your predicament without sacrifice. And for one of your friends, there will be no way out at all. You can't win. That is the definition of a no-win situation. The purpose of such a test lies not in finding the winning move despite apparent impossibility, but in losing with grace. It matters less what you choose and more how you go on afterward."

"But…" I objected again. "How can I possibly condemn one of my friends to death?"

"*Fate* has condemned them, Simon. Fate, and the choices of others, and their devotion to you, which made them follow you into peril in the first place. Fate condemns us all to death eventually."

"But I still have to choose?"

"Yes. Sometimes leaders must do that. It is easy to make the ultimate sacrifice yourself. Easy because it is quick. Harder to let someone else do it instead. You have to live with that gift forever. But, Simon, that is your role. You decide people's fate. It is the hardest thing in the world to resist the role that life has cast you to play. So don't. Just embrace it."

"But—" I began.

"No, we have talked enough. I have talked *too* much. The time has come for you to return."

101 How he rose to the stature of all-powerful, intergalactic super wizard without knowing who Captain Kirk was is a complete mystery. I still toss and turn over that one…

"But you could come back with me!" I said. "You could help me get the bloodstone from the draculadon and help me save all my friends. And help me defeat Rone, and—"

"Oh, no..." Xerith said, holding his hands up to stifle my words. "*You* are the hero of this story. There is no room for another. Besides, I'm old." He shifted painfully in the rocker, and his back popped loudly, illustrating his point. "My adventuring days are over. Even if I could go, I would not. My presence would only hinder your progress. Keep you from growing into the wizard your people need. Go now. Get the stone. Make your choice. And Simon?"

"What?" I said, dangling my finger over the seacup.

"You're going to need some new pockets..."

"Right."

I took one last look around the cabin. I glanced at the woods, the sea, the beach, the hills. "Xerith?"

"Yes, Simon?"

"Thanks."

He nodded. "Go. Be strong. Follow your code. Come back when you've done something interesting..."

"Like save the universe?"

"Like that. Come back after, and we'll talk about your future."

I grinned at him, then glanced down into the seacup. I could just make out Tessa and the Tike staring back at me. I stuck my finger into it, and the world exploded once more.

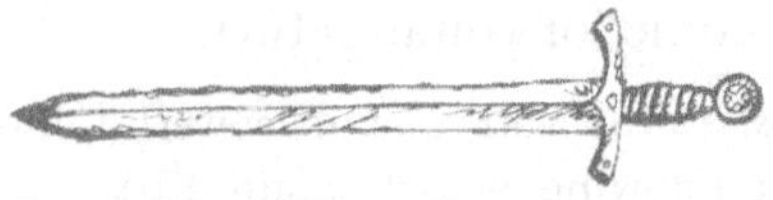

I materialized in the midst of a chamomile sea, with a

familiar door floating before me. I reached out, turned the handle, and pushed it open.

I fell out onto the grass in front of the broken shack that had started this whole mess and wiped tea from my face. It was nighttime now, but a full moon shone bright enough that I could see the blades of grass.[102] I rolled onto my back, turned E8 (*Stash*), and got to my feet as the girls appeared beside me.

"We're back outside!" Tessa exclaimed. "You did it! Did you meet him? Xerith, I mean? What did he say? What was he like?"

I pondered her questions. Of course, there was simply no way I was going to get close to repeating everything he had told me. "He was a bit weird," I said finally.

"Did he tell you how to defeat the draculadon?" Tessa said.

"Nope."

"Did he tell you what to do in the tomb of Rone?" the Tike asked.

"Nope."

Tessa sighed. "Good trip, then. Glad we did all that."

"Yep."

I looked at my friends: Tessa, with her legs gone, and friendship still strong between us. The Tike, with no idea what was going on around her, yet calm and cool, just glad to be by my side again.

"You guys are pretty cool," I said. "You know that?"

102 Funny how in life's big moments, you tend to notice the smallest things.

"I knew I was cool," Tessa said icily. "Didn't know I was a guy. You're *not* going to tell us what Xerith said, I take it?"

I shook my head.

"Well, I'll *make* you tell me later. We going back to Broca's? You've decided you want to try and get the bloodstone from the draculadon before Tav gets back?"

It wasn't a question. She could tell I'd made up my mind. Though I hadn't realized it myself until she mentioned it.

"Yes."

She nodded, stuck her hand back into the bindle cage, and I leaned down to throw her over my shoulder once more.

"Come on, ladies," I said. "Let's go see if that little dragon of ours has come up with a pla—"

The street shook, and I stumbled to my knees. The sound of distant screams filled the air, and the roar of what must have been a huge beast of some sort.

"What was that?" the Tike said.

"Look." Tessa pointed her tiny arm toward the center of the city.

I could just make out the tall, sparkling pyramid in the evening light. I could see now that the structure, which appeared white in the gleam of the sun, was actually transparent. It housed the ancient jaw-shaped arena—the Maw, from which the sounds were coming—and now that the sun had dipped behind the horizon, the transparent pyramid, lit from within, gleamed like a beacon at the center of the city. Even from here, I could see what was going on inside it. A cloud of red fire erupted into the air, rising out from between the toothlike projections that ringed the open circular roof of the arena. As the fire cleared, a gleaming white-and-purple dragon rose into the air, spun around, and dove back down out of sight.

"Oh no," I said.

"The draculadon!" Tessa exclaimed. "Tav must be fighting it."

"Come on!" I cried. "We have to get there before it's too late."

"Too late for what?" Tessa said, bouncing around in the bindle cage as I broke into a run. "What's your plan?"

"I don't know," I said.

"Simon," the Tike said as she ran beside me,[103] "it is unwise to rush into battle without a plan."

"You don't even know whose side you're going to be on," Tessa pointed out.

"Leto was going to..." I began. "We were supposed to—Argh!" I tripped over a stone and sprawled face forward into the street, scraping my hands on the ground.

"You dropped me!" Tessa shouted angrily.

The Tike picked up the bindle cage and slung it over her shoulder, helping me to my feet again.

"What are you going to do?" Tessa said as we started to run again.

"Don't worry so much, Tessa. I'll figure it out."

---

103 She could run forever and still carry on a conversation. No one should be in such good shape

"But what about the draculadon?" she shrilled.

"Tessa, I've got *you* to protect me."

That shut her up. I cursed silently as we ran. The Maw was growing steadily closer, but this was taking too long. Too bad I couldn't fly. I racked my brain for another option, mentally reviewing the turncoat diagram and the new knobs that I had memorized earlier. I almost chose C7 (*Gravity*) but settled on A8 (*Transportation*) instead. I didn't really expect it to work, since I had used it recently, but it seemed only logical to give it a chance. Even a pink bicycle would be better than running, and it would help me be less tired by the time I arrived. It's always nice to have a bit of energy left over for the actual fighting…

I turned the knob mentally, reveling in my newfound ability to do something that actually felt like magic. Next second, I was reclining in the cockpit of a bright-red Ferrari. The Tike, suddenly squished into the passenger's seat beside me, grunted in surprise.

"You really need to warn me before you do things like this, Simon," she said grumpily.

"Sorry," I said. I rolled down the window so that she could dangle Tessa's bindle cage out the side. The engine rumbled like a hungry lion.

"Do you know how to operate this machine?" the Tike said.

"Not really," I admitted, then jammed the gas pedal into the floor.

The price of becoming a new creature is the death of the old.

—Leto[104]

Drake stared blankly at the tiny dragon, unhearing. "Where's Simon?"

"Simon is about to be killed."

"WHAT?" Drake leaped forward, throwing himself against the bars.

"Ouch," Leto said. "That looked like it hurt."

"Why aren't you with him?" Drake said. "Protecting him."

"I need your help. There is a draculadon to fight tonight, Drakus. Not to mention several dozen wizards.

---

104 A Daruvian minor dragon, *Dracularus minutus*. One of the last and most famous examples of his race. Drakus Bright's noted historical work *Tarinea, City of Lights and Lies* reports that in his youth, Leto participated in the now infamous three-way clash of Titans that destroyed Tarinea, an event long thought to be the result of an asteroid strike or other celestial cataclysm. According to legend, Leto journeyed with Simon Fayter thousands of years later, living in the boy wizard's boot, though such tales are dismissed by most scholars as a wild invention of the famous wizard, who was widely known for shamelessly embellishing his own history.

He will not survive alone. Not this time."

"And Rone!" Drake said. "Rone is *here*, Leto! He's Tav. I mean, he was lying to us, and then he found this mask—*the* mask—the Jackal's mask, and he put it on, and… it was *him*.

"Yes," Leto said heavily. "Man is least himself when he talks in his own person. Give him a mask, and he will tell you the truth.[105]

"Go!" Drake said. "Go help him! I'm useless. We *both* know that you aren't!"

"Ah, yes." Leto rose to his tiny feet and stood on his hind legs. Completely upright, he was about two inches tall. "Simon fancies himself the genius, but *you* are the scholar, aren't you? You know the truth of my race."

Drake stared at his feet. "I might have found something in the library about you. *Dracularus minutus.* The Daruvian minor dragons. An ancient race. Thought to be nearly extinct. The only two surviving specimens live on Skelligard."

"Yes," Leto said. "Well, obviously that's not quite accurate."

"No."

"And what else did the book say?"

"Long life," Drake said, clearing his throat and quoting from memory. "In comparison to other members of the genus *Dracularus*, the *minutus* has an incredibly long life span, which is thought to be achieved through a

105 This is actually a quote from Oscar Wilde. Leto is very well read, it seems…

conservation of magical energy. The *minutus*'s true size, of course, is reported to be larger than even the draculadons of old. They are so large and powerful, it is said, that none could ever live a single minute beyond one thousand years, which is the ancient measure of a single day in the magic cycle of the universe.

"Regardless of health or other factors, a Daruvian minor dragon drops dead after exactly one thousand years spent in its normal body. Knowing this limitation, many specimens seem to spend the majority of their time inhabiting the miniature form in order to prolong their lives. Some of the older dragons are reported to have only a few days of natural life left and so have sworn to never take their full form again. As long as they do not, they live on indefinitely."

"You *memorized* the book?"

"Not the whole thing," Drake said, shrugging. "It seemed important."

"Well," Leto said, stroking his scaly chin with a clawed hand, "that is a surprisingly accurate account. I notice you did not give *that* book to Simon to read."

"I figured you would tell him if you wanted him to know."

"You *figured* correctly," Leto said. "Though, I imagine he will know after today."

"How long do you have left?" Drake asked.

"How much time can I spend in my own skin, you mean?" Leto growled, "Before I drop dead?" He hissed angrily, and Drake took a step back. "Quite a personal question."

"Sorry," Drake said. "It's just—"

"Five and a half minutes," Leto said.

Drake gaped. "F-five *minutes*?"

"Give or take."

"But—"

"Easier to see why I need your help now, isn't it? Assuming it will take more than five minutes to save Simon."

"But—"

"We have to go now, Drakus. The wizard Broca has removed the Groan from his lab and taken it to the Maw, as he always intended. He plans to make his would-be apprentices fight her there in front of the whole city. I have spoken with the draculadon imprisoned inside, you know. A young female. Young, as dragons think of these things. Thestraelin is her name. She came to Tarinea in search of her mother, who has not been seen since the city's founding six hundred years ago. Do you know the story of the founding, Drakus? The slaying of the great beast by Balgrotha the Wise?"

"Sure," Drake said. "Balgrotha came looking for a place to build the greatest city in the universe but found his chosen valley inhabited by a great beast. A Titan, the story says, though they do not specify what the nature of the monster was. Balgrotha constructed the Maw to look like the mouth of a great beast in honor of his victory. It's just a fable, though. So the books say."

"Truth lives in fables, Drakus. More often than you would expect. The Titan in question was a draculadon—the oldest, largest, and fiercest of its race. Thestraelin's mother, of course. *Her* name, is Bethangllowys, and she did not die. She was wounded, and she turned herself to stone. A defense mechanism of the draculadons, not unlike my own." He indicated his tiny form.

"Why are you telling me this?" Drake said.

"Because I am not the only one in Tarinea who knows fact from myth. Broca, who has long lived with one draculadon imprisoned in his basement, has determined that it would be foolish to harvest the starheart of such a small beast when he could use it as bait to lure out a full-grown specimen. As we speak, he is preparing to let his apprentices attempt to kill Thestraelin atop the frozen stone body of her mother. How do you think Bethangllowys will react to that?"

Drake had turned quite pale by now. "Simon—"

"Knows nothing of the situation he is walking into. I had to choose between warning him and fetching you. I made my choice. We must go now. I may have to fight to save him, this time. If Thestraelin's mother awakens, she will be truly full of fury."

"She'll try to kill Simon?" Drake said. "Why?"

"She'll destroy all of Tarinea, Drakus. If that happens, I may not be able to stop her." He squirmed uncomfortably. "Though I will try."

"But," Drake said, shaking his fists at his sides, "what good can I do? I guess you could break me out, if you wanted to transform in here, but what—"

"Are you going to eat that?" Leto pointed at the kulrakalakia. Drake still had it in his hand.

"*Eat* it?" Drake said. "That would kill me."

"Maybe," Leto said. "Maybe not. *Licking* it certainly hasn't had much effect. Besides, Drakus, the price of becoming a new creature is the death of the old. It has always been so."

Drake eyed the ball of green slime, thinking.

"Do not think too long. Simon's time grows short."

A second later, Drake's expression became suddenly fierce. Gone was the fearful youth. Need had replaced timidity within him, choking the life of it.

Drake set his jaw and ate the kulrakalakia in three big bites.

23 THE FIERY WRATH

In peace, nothing so becomes a man as modest stillness and humility: But when the blast of war blows in our ears, then imitate the action of the tiger; stiffen the sinews, summon up the blood, disguise fair nature with rage, and lend the eye a terrible aspect.

—Henry V[106]

"Wake up, Simon. Wake up!"

The Tike was shaking my shoulder.

"Wha? What happened?" I blinked, recovering my vision. I knew I was in the arena, for the bright light blazed down on me from above. The Ferrari was part slinky now, with bits of wreckage strewn across the floor.

"You really don't know how to operate that machine," the Tike said, helping me to my feet for the second time in five minutes. She still had Tessa's bindle cage over her shoulder, and it appeared to be intact. I shook my head, clearing my jumbled thoughts. I had driven straight at the side of the Maw, full speed ahead, and turned A3 (*Curse*) as I drove through the wall.

---

106 This is, in fact, another Shakespeare quote. It is from King Henry's famous speech which begins "Once more unto the breach, dear friends, once more." Clever readers will notice that I have altered it slightly to suit my purposes here.

No one seemed to have noticed our grand entrance, however. Far above us, they gasped and screamed as the great white dragon wove through the air in pursuit of Tav. At least, I thought it was Tav. He was far away, but he looked bigger than I remembered him, and he wore a long black cape and a mask that flashed golden under the arena's lights. Tav couldn't fly, could he? I mean, I didn't know him very well, but flying? That seemed a little too impressive, even for Tav.

As I stood there, wondering how to get into the fight—or better yet, *stop* the fight—a small sound caught my attention. I'm not sure how I heard it amid the chaos, but I did. It was a soft human sound, somewhere between a gurgle and a moan. I turned around, and there she was. Loni. Leaning against the outer wall, her face covered in blood.

"No!" I shouted, and rushed to her.

"I'm okay," she said when I reached her. "It's not as bad as it looks."

"We have to get you to a healer," I said.

"I am a healer," she said.

"You're covered in blood!"

"I have a head wound," she said, swaying a little. "They bleed a lot."

I caught her and laid her on the ground. The Tike tore the sleeve off her shirt and bound Loni's head.

"He's crazy, Simon," Loni said. "Tav. Crazy. Stole a spear from the king. Killed guards. I tried to stop him."

"Take her to get help," I said, turning to the Tike.

"Simon," the Tike said, "I won't leave you here to fight alone."

"Take her, Tike," I said. I felt my voice sharpen on the words. "Take her. Hurry back."

The Tike picked Loni up and ran toward the opening I'd made with the Ferrari. I strode into the center of the Maw and lit myself on fire.

It was an accident.

Sort of. I turned D6 (*Lightning*) because I had determined that the most important thing was to get everyone's attention, and it seemed like a bolt of lightning was just the thing. Unfortunately, my thoughts were so focused on drawing everyone's attention to myself that I must have drawn the lightning straight down on myself as well. So it was that my first act of battle was to blow myself ten feet into the air and set my pants on fire.

Still, it worked.

As soon as I recovered, I realized that both Tav and the dragon were barreling toward the ground. They struck the floor of the arena at the same time, sending up a cloud of dust. We were spaced equidistant, the three of us, though the dragon, being, you know, a dragon, seemed to take up more room. Its body was the size of two eighteen-wheeler's, and when it landed, the wind from its wings nearly knocked me down.

"Nice of you to show up," Tav called. "I thought you had given up for a while there."

"Nice cape, Tav!" I called, running toward him. "It lets you fly? That's awesome! Where'd you get it? Did you bring me one? Tav... Where'd you get that mask?"

As soon as I was close enough to see the Jackal's face, I felt a chill run down my spine. I had seen that mask before, but not on him.

"The mask I stole from the castle," Tav said. "The cape I borrowed from my brother, Rellik."

"No," I said, taking a step back. It wasn't possible. Was it? "Rone?"

"I found a weapon that can kill this thing, Simon. Are you going to help me or not?"

He twirled the spear, and I saw that it was much larger than I had expected. It was twelve feet long at least, and the metal shone brightly in the light of the Maw. The tip of the spear was stained with fresh blood. The draculadon looked fine, so whose was it? I thought of Loni. He stole a spear from the king. Killed guards. I thought of the blood all over her face.

"What happened to Loni, Tav?"

Tav laughed, spinning the spear. He advanced toward the draculadon, ignoring me. "She'll be all right, Simon. Come on. Help me kill this thing."

"What happened to Loni, Rone? And what did you do to Drake? WHAT DID YOU DO TO DRAKE, YOU MONSTER?"

Rone slammed the butt of the spear into the ground angrily. "I did what I had to do. If you don't want to help me, fine. But stay out of my way. Don't think I won't kill you just because we're connected in the future. I'm willing to take my chances."

He spun away, racing toward the draculadon, and the great beast opened its mouth, sending a torrent of red fire at him. He leaped upward and flew over it, but the draculadon swatted him out of the air. Tav hit the ground hard, rolling sideways. He was on his feet a second later, spear held high.

I drew Kylanthus and spoke its name in my mind, lighting the blade. "Tav!" I cried. "Rone! You don't have to do this. You don't have to become…you. It's not too late to turn back."

The draculadon lurched forward, and Rone spun to the side. The beast stomped down, gouging the earth with its huge claws.

"That's your problem," Tav said. "You think I want to turn back. I never wanted to turn back, Simon. I know what I'm becoming. I know better now that you've told me." He darted forward and lunged with the spear, burying it deep into the beast's pale foot.

The draculadon roared in rage, flinging Tav away like a discarded action figure. It curled forward and grabbed the spear with its teeth, ripping it out.

Then it leveled its electric blue eyes on me. Its jaws slapped shut, and the spear snapped in half and tumbled to the ground.

"Oh, hey," I said, in my most dragonsoothingest[107] voice. "I'm not going to hurt you. And you're not going to eat me, right? Right? RIGHT?"

The draculadon opened its mouth wide, and I yelped,

---

107 Not a word.

breaking into a run. I reached into the turncoat for a knob. Any knob. I'd quite forgotten that I could turn them with my mind. I just wanted something to happen right now. But there wasn't time. The draculadon exhaled a burst of golden fire (Wait a minute. *Golden* fire? Hadn't it been red just a second ago?).

I felt the warmth of that fire only briefly. It didn't burn me to death. It didn't kill me.

The second it touched me, it disappeared. In fact, everything disappeared. The arena, the draculadon, Tav, everything. I was standing inside a golden diamond. At least, that's how I'm going to describe it poetically. It's pretty hard to describe what the starheart of a draculadon looks like from the inside. The floor was gold, and not at all flat. The walls shimmered, and I was pretty sure I could taste them as well as see them. That was weird.

I wasn't alone. A girl stood there. Not the young child I had seen inside the Groan, but a young woman, eighteen, with skin white as the draculadon, hair of purple and green—like its wings—and electric blue eyes.

"Hi there," I said.

"Simon Fayter?" the girl said slowly. She had a thick accent, and I almost didn't recognize the sound of my own name. "You have come to help?"

"Well, I'm trying to," I said.

She nodded, sitting down in a chair. There was a chair there as soon as she sat on it.

"This is a very strange place," I pointed out.

"Thank you," she said, smiling. "It is my starheart. It

is where I live. Do humans live inside their hearts? I have never understood this?"

"Uhh…"

"Leto says you do. He says you will come to help me. And here you are."

"Well," I said, "Leto knows a lot of stuff that I don—"

"My name is Thestraelin. I have kept safe for you that which another wished to hide. You may take it now, but you must also help me. Broca wants my starheart."

"Yeah," I said. "I mean, thanks. Sorry about the killing-you-for-your-heart thing. I'll do my best to, you know, help you ou—"

"But that is not his secret goal."

"His secret goa—"

"His secret goal is to wake my mother. Bethangllowys."

"You don't really let a guy finish a sentence, do you?" I noted. "Your moth—"

"She lies beneath the ground here, encased in living stone. She will wake soon, sensing that I am in danger. She will be angry. She will destroy this world. She will die. She sleeps because she does not have the energy to wake and also live."

"Okay," I said, holding up a hand. "I'm really glad that you and Leto came to some sort of an agreement, but you are really confusing me now. Why don't you just tell me what you want me to d—"

"Fight with me!" she cried, rising to her feet. "Help me, Simon Fayter! Do not let them kill me!"

"Them?" I said. "Who's th—"

The vision ended as suddenly as it had begun. I rose into the air with a sudden burst of speed, sitting astride the white dragon, my legs straddling the crook of its neck. Below us, I saw Tav flying upward. He was holding the now normal-sized spear in his hands.

But he hadn't reached us yet.

Right in front of me, a thick golden chain wound around Thestraelin's neck. I knew exactly what was hanging on the other end, too. The clasp was right in front of me, and strangely, it looked not unlike the clasp of a regular girl's necklace. Of course, this necklace probably weighed about twelve hundred pounds, so the clasp was a bit too much for me to handle.[108] Keeping my head, however, I sheathed Kylanthus and turned B6 (*Strength*) with my mind, hoping that it would turn me into Superman.

In an unprecedented display of non-shocking-randomness,[109] the turncoat did exactly what I expected it to do:[110] It made me stronger. I undid the clasp, swung

108 If we're being honest, girl's necklace clasps, even regular-sized ones, are too much for most men to handle in the best of circumstances.

109 Not a word.

110 It turned me into Superman. My eyes sprouted laser beams, my skin took on the properties of ivory-colored Kevlar, and I gained the strength of ten thousand men. I flew around the planet so fast that I changed the direction of its rotation, which somehow also took me back in time to Chicago, on Black Friday, 1961. There, I burst into Macy's department store, bought all the red underwear I could find (red tighties, I call them), and began wearing them on the outside of my pants. Okay... You caught me. The knob didn't really do that. That would be absurd, and we don't want anything absurd in this

the chain in a high arc, and turned E8 (*Stash*), depositing the whole thing, bloodstone and all, into the turncoat.[111]

I must have taken my sweet time doing all that, by the way, because when I glanced back up, Tav's spear was about three feet from my face and closing fast. I turned B9 (*Luck*), and the spear tip just barely missed my nose. How lucky is that?

I grabbed the haft and pulled, wrenching Tav out of his orbit. I caught him by the throat and hurled him away from us in a hundred-foot arc. It was pretty awesome having super strength. Too bad it only lasted ten seconds…

When he came back, I tried the same thing again and was smashed in the head for my trouble. Super strength doesn't last forever. He struck out at us again, but Thestraelin drove him off with fire.

We twisted in the air to pursue Tav, and something caught my eye on the ground.

It was Broca.

He strode into the arena with an air of calm determination, as if everything was going according to plan. He raised a great black crossbow and fired.

I'll admit, when I first spotted the crossbow, I wasn't overly concerned. What could a weapon that size do against something like Thestraelin? But something strange happened when he fired it. The crossbow bolt grew. It grew and it grew the closer it came to us. In the first second of travel, the arrowhead grew from being the

---

book (except for chapters 4, 13, 19, and 21).

111 The E8 pocket must have a weight rating over 1400 lbs, because it didn't throw off my balance at all.

size of, well, an arrowhead, to being the size of a mini fridge. In the second second[112] of flight, it grew to the size of a cruise missile. When it struck Thestraelin, it tore her left wing clean off.

Now, before you completely freak out, let me assure you that in their anatomical makeup, draculadons are less like birds and more like insects, by which I mean that while Thestraelin was in a great deal of pain, and she couldn't fly anymore, her life wasn't directly threatened by this loss.

We did, however, tumble out of the air. Right before we hit the ground, I turned C7 (*Gravity*)[113] and hoped beyond hope that it would have the type of effect that I desired. I didn't know much about how to control the C7 knob back then, so I was pleasantly surprised when Thestraelin's descent slowed dramatically, and we hit the ground as if we had fallen from twenty feet rather than three hundred.

I turned B1 (*Leap*) and leaped down from Thestraelin's back, taking up a defensive position between her and Broca. He raised the crossbow again and fired.

I turned D7 (*Disarm*), and the arrow exploded in a flash of light.[114] The crossbow cracked into three separate pieces and tumbled to the ground in a heap.

---

112 Yes. I did that on purpose. Second second.

113 You have to admire how good I was under pressure. Most people have trouble remembering lists, maps, diagrams, and other random information when they are tumbling through the air in a dragon-sponsored death spiral. Not me, though.

114 I was actually shocked at this. I had expected his arms to fall off.

"Yahoo!" I shouted, jumping up and down like an idiot.[115]

I turned around to check on Thestraelin, and Tav's spear shot through my chest. It passed straight through the middle, exploding in my heart and skewering me to the earth.

"Oops," I whispered as blood began to trickle from the corners of my mouth. My vision went dark, and just before my brain died from lack of oxygen, I did a quick mental inventory of the turncoat knobs and used my last bit of willpower to turn A9 (*Do-Over*). Obviously I didn't know what would happen, but I figured if I ever needed a do-over, it was now. Also, I didn't have much to lose.

Right before we hit the ground, I turned C7 (*Gravity*) and hoped beyond hope that it would have the type of effect that I desired. I didn't know much about how to control the C7 knob back then, so I was pleasantly surprised when Thestraelin's descent slowed dramatically, and we hit the ground as if we had fallen from twenty feet rather than three hundred.

I shook my head, experiencing a very powerful déjà vu. Then it hit me. This wasn't déjà vu. I had traveled back in time. About ten seconds, it seemed.

I turned B1 (*Leap*) and leaped down from Thestraelin's back, taking up a defensive position between her and Broca. I ducked and rolled, searching the air for Tav. He was above and behind me. I locked eyes with him, while

---

115 I often shout the names of random internet search engines when I'm excited. It's a rare form of Tourette Syndrome.

behind me, I knew, Broca raised the crossbow and fired. I turned D7 (*Disarm*) while keeping the spear, the crossbow, and the bolt firmly in my focus. The arrow exploded in a flash of light. The crossbow cracked into three separate pieces and tumbled to the ground in a heap. The head of Tav's spear fell off, and the shaft crumbled to dust in his hands.

"Yahoo!"[116] I shouted, jumping up and down like an idiot.

Thestraelin roared. Then she spun in a tight circle, breathing fire as she did, so that for a moment we were surrounded on all sides by a wall of red flame.

When the fire subsided, Tav was walking toward us, stomping out the tattered remains of his cloak. His mask was gone, and his face was stained black with smoke. Broca was there too, his smallsword in hand, and it was pointed directly at me. In the other hand, he held the head of the spear.

"Tough to kill a draculadon," Broca said. "Very tough. I managed to make this"—he kicked the remains of the crossbow—"my Winglance. But it wouldn't have killed her anyway. Not completely." He raised the spear head, testing the weight of it in his hand. "This should."

"Let me do it," Tav said.

Broca laughed. "It seems my true apprentice has revealed himself. But no, boy. We will take them together. You get the boy. I'll get the beast."

Thestraelin unleashed fire again.

---

116 See? Tourette syndrome.

Broca wasn't ready for it. He raised his sword and screamed, but when the fire dissipated, he was gone.

"Dang!" I said. "Good job, Thestraelin!"

"First rule of warfare," Broca said from behind me. "Never be where your enemy expects."

I whipped around to find him standing right beneath Thestraelin's chest, just out of eyesight. Her head jerked down too, and her mouth opened wide. But he was too quick for her.

The second her jaws parted, the spear head sparked with fire. It grew larger in his hand, longer, like a lengthening shadow. He threw it up at her, and it shot with the speed of an arrow, right down her gullet. Her eyes went wide, and the gleam went out of them. I watched it happen. Her head rocked back, and her long neck slapped down against the earth, sending up a plume of dust.

"No!" I said, running to her side. "Thestraelin?"

I couldn't hear her breathing anymore.

It was too much. Loni. Drake. And now Thestraelin. I screamed, throwing myself at Broca.

He held up a hand, palm out, and my body froze in midair.

"Take it from him," he hissed. "Quickly."

And before I could think or reach for a knob mentally, Tav caught hold of the turncoat and ripped it off me.

"Give that to me," Broca said, and Tav tossed it over. He tucked it under one arm and walked to Thestraelin's side. He bent down, listening. As he did, he released me from his spell, and I slipped forward onto my own two legs. "This one's still breathing," he said, "but only just. Another minute or two. You finish the boy off, and I'll try to retrieve the spear. You did good, finding the weapon."

Tav looked at me, and I could see the triumph in his eyes. But there was something else there too.

I backed away from him, heading for the edge of the arena. "You don't have to do this," I said. "I can tell you don't want to."

Tav wiped blood from the corner of his mouth. "As usual, Simon, I'll do what I have to do."

We began to circle each other, and soon his back was to the wall of the arena. He stopped suddenly, standing up a little taller. "Of course," he said, "you could always join us instead..."

I laughed. "I don't think so." I reached into my pocket and drew out my ear. I threw it at him, and to my delight, it hit him in the face.

"Ugh!" he said. He stomped on my ear, grinding it into the dust. "What's wrong with you?"

"I'm a good person," I said, "that's what. This happened to me because I wasn't being my best self. Because I gave up." I indicated the earless holes in the sides of my head. "Can you imagine what would happen to me if I abandoned my morals entirely and joined my archenemy in a campaign to destroy the world?"

I spat in the dirt. "No thank you. It's time I stopped running away. I'm going to beat you today. Somehow. I'm going to beat you. Then I'm going to go back to the future and let you *think* you've beaten me. But just remember.

Remember, hundreds of years from now, when we meet in your tomb, that I'm not beaten. You can't control me. You can't destroy me. I will get you in the end."

He opened his left hand, palm up. With his right, he drew a thin black dagger from his belt. "How would you like to die?" he said. "Magic? Or the old-fashioned way?"

I sighed, feeling the fury of the previous moment fizzle out of me. "Magic," I said. "Duh. Who wants to get stabbed?"

He grinned, raising the knife.

He never got to use it, though, for at that moment, something large and hairy burst through the arena wall with the speed of a spellbound Ferrari. A huge minotaur thrashed through the tumble of rock and dust. It was eight feet tall, with hands as thick as tractor tires. It picked Tav up like a sack of potatoes and raised him into the air.

"Break him in half, Drakus," a deep voice said, and the minotaur took one of Tav's legs in each hand and ripped them apart. There was a loud *crack*, and Tav fell to the ground, unconscious, his hip bones cracked in half. The Jackal's gold mask tumbled to the ground, and Drake bent to pick it up.

While I stood there, mouth hanging open in shock, Tav's body zoomed across the ground and came to rest next to Broca, who placed a hand on his shoulder. His hand flashed, and Tav shifted slightly, starting to breathe again. Broca's right arm was covered in black slime now, and he held the spear head once more.

"Vicious beast," the wizard spat, addressing the

minotaur. "You have broken my new apprentice. It will take me weeks to mend him properly. No matter..." Broca turned and plunged the spear head into Thestraelin, glancing around at the arena as he did so. "Come," he mumbled to himself. "Rise! I'm killing her."

He plunged it in again, and Thestraelin groaned, rolling over.

The ground shook.

The arena walls shifted slightly, cracking. People fell screaming from the stands while others ran for the exits.

Above us, several of the bright lights flickered out, and I looked up. Beyond the toothlike projections at the top of the Maw, moonlight shone through the clear top of the pyramid.

"It is happening, Drakus," the deep voice said. "Get Simon to safety!"

I saw the source of the voice then. It was a little orange gecko. It sat perched in between the massive minotaur's horns, holding on to the thick hair with both fists.

"Leto?" I said, perplexed.[117] "Where did you find that minotaur? Have you seen Drake anywhere? I think—" My voice choked a bit here. "I think Tav might have killed him."

"It's me, genius!" the minotaur boomed. Leto flew into the air and rose slowly upward, beating his tiny wings.

---

117 By the way, you are probably wondering about the holes in Leto's story, like how his conversation with Thestraelin went, how he escaped the Titan's Groan, how he decided to help Drake instead of me, and how he and Drake escaped the castle. I wonder about that too. Unfortunately, he never told me. Dragons...

Above us, the toothlike protrusions at the apex of the arena walls were developing surface cracks. Stone and dust fell away from them, leaving actual teeth behind.

I glanced at Broca, who was standing with his mouth slightly open, eyebrows raised in surprise.

"Simon," the minotaur said, "we are standing in the mouth of a giant draculadon."

I gaped at him. "Drake?"

"It's Thestraelin's mother."

"Buddy, is that you?"

"She froze herself in stone because she doesn't have the energy to stay alive, but now she's going to sacrifice herself to save her daughter. It's all part of Broca's plan."

"It *is* you, Drake! Holy *cow*, dude! You weren't kidding when you said minotaurs do puberty fast![118]

"Simon, if we stay here, we will be eaten." He gestured wildly with the Jackal's mask, indicating the arena at large.

Near the center of the floor, the hard-packed dirt was beginning to sink down, as if the throat of the beast was beginning to open. I didn't really notice, though. I was still fixated on Drake's sudden transformation.

"Your biceps are like the size of Shetland ponies!"

"Okay," he said, and threw me over his shoulder. "Clearly you hit your head or something. Try to pay attention. I need to tell you something about Leto." He shouted as he ran, and I only caught half of what he said. Something about Leto having five minutes to live and

118 Please excuse my language. I was, at this point, somewhere between bumfuzzlement, flabbergastation, and shockwollop.

secretly being huge. It didn't make much sense. When he reached the opening he had come in by, Drake stopped short. The ground on the other side was falling away fast, as if the arena[119] was rising into the air.

Above us, there was a huge crashing noise as the top of the arena burst through the pyramid and rose into the night sky.

"Whoa," I said. "That's weird. You know, I bet we'll be okay. I'd be safer if I had the turncoat, but I think I can make that drop."

"Good," Drake said. "You get to safety, I'll get the turncoat." And he tossed me out.

I fell about fifteen feet and rolled down the side of a slanting piece of rock that buckled up against the face of the rising draculadon.[120]

I turned and stared at the rising mass of rock in utter disbelief. How could anything so big be alive?

I ran then, as hard as I could. I had realized, of course, that I had only seen the face and neck emerge so far, and the body would have to follow. I ran and ran, but I didn't run nearly far enough. The ground broke apart and surged into the air, spreading into a gargantuan set of wings. They beat downward with a sound like the earth itself shattering, and the whole thing accelerated. When the dust cleared, I was sitting on the back of an immense black dragon, a mile long from tip to tail, with skin of hard black stone. The dust and dirt that had encapsulated

---

119 When I say *arena* here, I clearly mean *dragon mouth.*

120 Thanks a lot, Drake. Thank goodness I was young and scrappy, or I might not have walked away from that one.

the beast for so long now hung in the night air, glistening like fog in the moonlight. Something black and furry fell toward me out of the sky, and Drake nearly killed me *again*—this time by landing on top of me.

"Are you okay?"

"Half of me is," I groaned.

"I got the turncoat. Broca is a bit busy right now, so he didn't notice."

"I bet. Bit off a little more than he could chew, huh?"

"A bit." He glanced around, taking in our situation. "What do you think?"

"I think we get the heck off this thing as soon as possible."

"Right. How?"

"Here," I said. I jumped on his back, then climbed onto his shoulders like a toddler. "Okay. Now, hold on to my legs and jump off."

"Simon!"

"It'll be okay. You might have to tuck that mask away somewhere. Why are you keeping it? You hoping if we steal it, he won't be able to become the Jackal? I don't think that's going to wor—"

"It might be useful!" Drake snapped, tucking the mask inside his cloak. "I mean— Gah! This is no time to chat! It's like a three-thousand-foot drop!"

"And it's only getting higher. Jump!"

Drake howled and took a running leap, flinging us into space. For the split second that elapsed between jumping off and starting to fall, I took in the scene before us: Moon above, the lights of Tarinea spread out below like a growing patchwork quilt, and an unspeakably large mass of rocklike dragon untangling itself in the distance between us. I couldn't believe how high we were already. It really *was* like three thousand feet down.

We started to fall. I turned B1 (*Leap*) and nothing happened. I guess I had used that one recently.

I turned C7 (*Gravity*), and nothing happened. Huh. Come to think of it, I had used *that* one recently as well. Oops…

I did a mental inventory as we plummeted to our deaths and decided that C10 (*Inflation*) was probably our best bet. I turned it, and then I sort of…ballooned.

I felt pretty normal, but Tessa told me afterward that from the ground I looked like a giant hot-air balloon. It took us a solid minute to float to the ground, as apparently I am full of more hot air than you might think.

Unfortunately, my head was at the top of this Simon balloon, and it sort of got sucked down so tight that I was staring straight up at the sky. This meant that I had a pretty good view of a giant dragon butt, which also meant I had no idea where we were going.

Drake shouted directions up at me from time to time, and after thirty seconds or so, took to pulling my legs one way or the other, steering us through the air. When we landed, I turned C7 again, and once I was back to normal size, I made Drake swear never to tell anyone about it, which of course was completely pointless since half of Tarinea had seen it happen.

Drake tapped me on the shoulder when I was done ranting, and I turned around to see a thing that I will never forget: The largest known dragon in the history of the universe descending on Tarinea in fiery wrath.

Although the world is full of suffering, it is full also of the over-coming of it.

—Helen Keller[121]

The draculadon's fire was black. Black as the rotten soul of midnight's shadow. Dark as the Vale of Nightmares.[122] So black that it made the night sky look bright by comparison.

The first waves of flame consumed a full quarter of Tarinea. Thankfully, it was the graveyard quarter.[123]

The dragon twisted, and I could see it raise one hand and lift something small and white upon its shoulder. Thestraelin.

It was still defending its daughter. Tarinea had done this to them, the dragon no doubt thought, and Tarinea would pay.

---

121 Helen Keller knew whereof she spoke. When she was nineteen months old, she became both deaf and blind. She later went on to become the first deaf-blind person to earn a bachelor's degree and is now well-known the world over for her positive attitude and perseverance.

122 Yes. There is such a place. We go there in Book 5.

123 Still, think of how many dead people that probably killed.

The draculadon lurched, preparing to release another bout of flame, and then another thing happened that I will never forget: A sound like ten thunders ripped across the sky, and Leto appeared, blocking out the moon. He was a full half-mile long himself, and he did not hold back.

He rammed the draculadon with all his might, turning her around. The larger dragon spun away and turned, letting fly a gout of black flame a thousand feet wide, and Leto's fire met it, blue against black, lighting up the night like an unexpected sunrise. They were two miles away, but the heat from their fire made me sweat where I stood.

Someone screamed my name, and I turned. It was the Tike, limping toward me with Tessa slung over her shoulder in the bindle cage. She drew up next to me and gaped at the dragons, mumbling something in her native language and covering the white oval on her cheek with the palm of her hand.

The dragons grappled with each other, claws catching claws, still pointing their streams of fire into each other's faces. Something happened then, to the fire. Rather, to the place the two fires met: It grew brighter and brighter, like a star, until it was as bright as noonday around us. Then it seemed to take on a life of its own. The star fire erupted downward in a vast pillar, opening the ground and burning down, down to the center of the earth. Another quarter of the city swelled and bubbled with the heat. Houses rose into the air and exploded. Whole neighborhoods sunk in melting craters, glowing with red heat as the darkness of night descended once more.

I looked on in horror and sudden realization hit me. Tarinea wasn't destroyed by an asteroid. It wasn't destroyed by magical war either. It was this. It was us. It was because I had come.

I had come, and now it was chaos. People were dying. Children screamed.

Seeing the destruction that the fire was causing, Leto broke free and fled, turning his back to the draculadon. It attacked him from behind, bathing his back in fire, but he flew on toward us.

Leto's voice boomed above the noise of the fire, above the screams of the city: "RUN, TARINEANS! EMPTY THE CITY. I CANNOT STOP HER. I CANNOT STOP HER!"

"Stay close," I told the others. "We're going to leave now. The moment Leto transforms, we're going to leave."

"How long has it been?" Drake shouted in my ear. "Since Leto transformed. Two minutes? Three?"

"What? Why?"

Leto's shadow fell across us, and I could feel the warmth of the dragon fire as it lit up his back.

"Wait," Drake was saying, looking around wildly. "Loni! Loki! We can't leave them here. We can't leave them here to…to—"

Leto landed on top of us, protecting us from the barrage of fire with his back. The flames came on and on, bathing him, until finally they stopped for a brief moment. In that moment, Leto was gone. Or rather, he was sitting on my shoulder, trailing a tiny cloud of smoke. I looked at him.

"Run, Simon," he whispered. "It's over." Then he skittered down my body and into my boot.

Above us, the draculadon's fire erupted again, streaming toward the ground. It struck a thousand yards off, and the earth heaved and bubbled. A wall of flames shot toward us, and the sound of screaming filled my ears again.

I put my arms around my friends, bowed my head against the heat, and turned E7.

Geoffrey: *"You chivalric fool…as if the way one fell down mattered."*

Richard the Lionheart: *"When the fall is all that's left, it matters a great deal."*

—James Goldman, *The Lion in Winter*[124]

We rematerialized on the other side of the universe, deep underground, in the tomb of Rone. Above us, hundreds of bloodhounds scrambled over the invisible dome of the soultrap, dropping one by one through the widening hole at its apex.

The Tike whirled into action, catching one of the evil beasts by the throat and hurtling it away from us. Captain Bast stuck his sword through another. Hawk destroyed a third. They were keeping up, but not for long.

---

124 This is actually a *misquotation*. The exact lines are slightly different, but these are better. They were quoted this way by one of my favorite United States presidents, Josiah Bartlet. James Goldman, by the way, was an Academy Award-winning screenwriter and brother to William Goldman, *also* an Academy Award-winning screenwriter (*Butch Cassidy and the Sundance Kid, All the President's Men*) as well as a novelist (*The Princess Bride, Marathon Man*). *The Lion in Winter* is a 1968 film about the Plantagenet kings starring Anthony Hopkins (his film debut).

The dome cracked, and thirty bloodhounds fell down together. Bast and Hawk and the Tike flew to my side, forming a tight defensive circle around me. Drake was there too, horns lowered, sling raised. Tessa, whose legs were seamlessly joined to her torso once more, took my hand. Her eyes caught mine, and though the noise of the dogs and the fighting made talking impossible, I knew what she was telling me: It's okay.

I released her hand, closed my eyes, and turned E2 (*Pause*). At the same instant, I reached out and caught Bast by the shoulder. The world stopped for everyone but us. I watched him lurch in surprise as the dogs he battled stopped moving. He tugged his sword free from one of them and looked around, confused.

"Captain," I said.

"Aye?" He turned and found me.

"I stopped time for us," I explained. "Just for a few seconds."

"Ah." His voice became gruff. "Ye've made yer decision, then." He lowered his head, looking me dead in the eyes. "I'm ready."

He took a step back from me and twirled his sword restlessly, but his eyes never left mine. "Try not to feel too bad 'bout it. It was me time."

"I won't forget your bravery," I said, feeling my voice catch.

He shook his head. "Ain't no such thing as bravery. Jus' hearts more filled up with love than fear."

I raised a hand in farewell and spoke the words I had

once heard him say at the death of another: "Godspeed, my brother. May your soul find rest among the stars."

"Aye-aye, Cap'n." Bast swung his sword in a salute, then turned away from me, facing the oncoming crowd of bloodhounds. He looked determined to fight till the end, despite the odds. I expected nothing less of him.

I pulled the others into a tight group, wrapping my arms around the four of them—Hawk, Tessa, Drake, the Tike—holding them as tightly as I could. I glanced over my shoulder at Bast, standing patiently, waiting for the end. I looked past him to Rone, dark eyes frozen in a wicked stare from behind the Jackal's mask.

Then I mentally turned E6 (*Travel*), and the awful scene winked out of existence.

The woods are lovely, dark and deep
But I have promises to keep,
And miles to go before I sleep,
And miles to go before I sleep.

—Robert Frost[125]

The woods were silent.

I landed with my face in the cold white snow.

"No," Hawk was saying. "No. Who did he leave? Tike? Where are you? Bast?"

I lifted my head out of the snow and saw a forest glade, pale and sparkling under a full moon. The sounds of the night were hushed by a thick blanket of snow. All I heard was the rustling and confused voices of my friends.

"Tessa?" That was Drake.

"I'm here."

"Are you—"

"My legs are back, Drake. I'm all right."

"Where is the Tike?" Hawk asked again. He was on his feet now.

---

125 A famous nineteenth-century San Franciscan poet. His best-known poem is probably "The Road Not Taken." He won *four* Pulitzers.

"I'm here," the Tike said, climbing out of a snowbank and brushing herself off.

"Bast?" Hawk called again.

"Bast?" Tessa said.

"He's gone," I said, rising to my feet, and the woods went silent once more.

I turned to look at them. Hawk hung his head, massaging his temples, as if he could get the heavy thoughts out that way. The Tike was holding Drake, who had begun to sob, his huge new minotaur body shaking. Tessa was watching me. She took a step toward me, concern written across her face, and I turned my back to her.

I had no more words in me. No more feelings. For me, the tears would not come. I had no comfort to give my friends in their grief, nor did I have any clear thoughts or answers—no wisdom or certainty to give my own mind peace. So I turned my back and walked. Walked away into the trees of…wherever we were now. To be alone.

My friends were loud in their sadness. My insides somehow loud in their confusion and emptiness. The past was loud, shouting in my heart of friends suddenly long dead. Of Tarinea destroyed by evil men, and my own ignorance, and the wicked twists of fate. The future was loud too, howling need and duty in my mind like freezing mistrals,[126] speaking of Rone, of sacrifices yet unmade, of bloodstones yet unfound. One of those bloodstones, no doubt, was hidden somewhere on this new snow-covered world.

---

126 Mistral: a strong, cold wind. Especially from the northwest.

Everything was loud. So I walked, alone, into the woods.

And the woods were silent.

Thank you to…

…My beta readers: Spencer Bowen, Spencer Bagshaw, and Hailey Walton.

…To God.

…And to my launch team, upon whom I depend:

Patti Anderson
April Angel
Sonia Arroyos
Terri Arturi
Candice Aucamp
Katie Babbit
Angel Barraza
Lydia Barron
Julie Bennett
Karen Bennett
Melanie Bessas
Jeanine Bevacqua
Bry Boler
Melissa Bonaparte
Rachel Bonnichsen
Randall Booth
Sofia Bostrom
Daniele Bourhis
Alisha Bowen
Riche Boyce
John Chasteen
Suzanne Christensen
Rachel Church
Amanda Comrie
Emma Curtis
Brandy Dalton
Janice David
Tom Davidson
Maureen Davlin
Bryan Deal
Brandy Emmert
Charlie Evans
Roger Fauble
Jennifer Firestone

Sarah Flint
Shannon Forslund
Danielle Foster
Jamie Francke
Sierra Furrow
Jennifer Fury
Bradley Gartin
Kisara Gibbons
Carmen Gomez
Daniel Grala
Mike Grant
Charlene Greene
Phil Gulbrandsen
Elva Guzman
Linda Hansen
Riley Harlan
Bruce Hastie
Shirley Holten
Claudia Howard
Jody Huffman
Sara Ingles
Krista Jasper
Bonnie Keck
Richard Kellerman
Manie Kilian
Emily Killgo
Keith Klayh
Jennifer Lapachian
Tiffany Lawrence
Georganne Lynch
Khyla Malone
Arisleny Martinez
John Maxim
Marilee McQuarrie
Veronica Meidus-Heilpern
Joyce Michelmore
Candace Miller
Michael Minkove
Becky Modderman
Mary Moffatt
James Morrow
Cathy Mulcahey
Shirlee Nicol
Debbie Nix
Anna Olsen
Daria Peterson
Eva Pontious
Isaac Reyes
Nicky Robinson
Angela Ross
Kari Schick
Britton Schwartz
Shelly Sessions
Crystal Shapiro
Michelle Shelton
Leena Smith
Lauren Smith
Eileen Smith

Jim Stavast
David Thorp
Aiden Tombuelt
Cheryl Torricer
Chelsea Tracy
Lana Turner
Stacey Valdez
Maria Wetherbee
Kelly Williams
Deidre Williams
Liz Wilson
Ron
Jeanine
Shari
Anna
Tanya
Robin
Karen